# The Fevered Hive

## By Dennis Lewis

Published by Accent Press Ltd – 2005
www.accentpress.co.uk

ISBN 095486736X

Printed and bound in the UK
by Clays, St Ives Plc.

Cover Design by Rachel Loosmore
Accent Press Ltd.

With support from the
Welsh Book Council.

To Helen: For teaching me all I know about friendship.

# Contents

Introduction

Prodigals and Puritans                          1

Colours Of The Moon                            11

Fanatics                                       29

The Cupboard Wife                              41

The Fevered Hive                               49

Goodnight Golgotha                             57

Phrenics, Gluggers and Fabulists               67

The Love Disease                               81

The Corrupted                                  93

The Other Side                                111

Revenge                                       121

Kevin's Youth                                 135

Run!                                          147

Davey's Oak                                   157

Wales Forever?                                167

Blind Date                                    177

# Introduction

At first glance, it may seem that the only thing that a social worker in Cardiff has in common with a City dealer in London is income tax. But the likelihood is that both are suffering the perdition of stress, are struggling to buy a house and feel threatened by job loss and violence on the streets. It is also likely that both are familiar with loneliness and despair, a product of the social atomization that city living produces. According to statistics, it is also increasingly likely that they have both tried illegal drugs.

The flamboyant characters and curious manners of a particular region provide fertile grounds for practitioners of urban writing. All fiction feeds on specificity, so it seems to me that the very best urban fiction has always been regional. The stories contained in this book are rich with the lateral dramas of locally inspired characters, but their various stories can be replaced by a single vertical drama: regional specificity succumbing to human generality.

Welcome to my city.

Dennis Lewis 2005

# Prodigals and Puritans

Lewis was in the Outpatient Department at the University Hospital, having another cosy chat with Dr Rosen. She gave him a prickly feeling all down his spine, did Dr Rosen, and it was nothing to do with him being ill. This particular tingle was to do with being a man. Dr Rosen was a train-stopping beauty.

It seemed Lewis had only just made it to middle-age. He had entered his forties with a casualty ward of medical problems, the biggest worry being his liver. (How do the French say, a *crise de foie?*) According to the medics, it was an hepatic 'Sword of Damocles'. (Lewis called it a 'Sword of DoasIplease'.)

"Let's just convert that into units, Mr Lewis," Doctor Rosen was saying. She scribbled unhappily on her pad, her lips pursed in the effort of calculation. He knew it wouldn't be good news. It seemed strange to be calling her 'Doctor' when she looked as though she'd only just qualified from being a teenager into womanhood. The lovely Dr Rosen looked eighteen but had to be in her late twenties.

"That's still too much, Mr Lewis. Way too much. You're still doing damage to yourself." Apparently (according to the ultra-sound scanner whose insides started life trying to detect lurking submarines and now sat triumphantly in the corner, harbouring its all-seeing eye) Lewis's liver was too 'big'. It was also too 'bright' and, to his utter dismay, too 'echogenic'. It was starting to feel like something as big as a ship reposed beneath his ribs, deplorably nudging aside other organs as if they were miniature icebergs. This was not good. This, in fact, combined with the results of the blood tests, was potentially disastrous. During a quiet moment, when the doctor scribbled in her notes, Lewis struggled to listen to his liver, its teeming alleyways groaning and creaking, crying out for relief. "FOR GOD'S SAKE STOP DRINKING!" screamed and echoed around its throbbing, life-giving plumbing.

"It'll have to stop, Mr Lewis. Completely. I don't mean cut down. I mean no more. Or it will certainly KILL YOU. If you carry on drinking like this you'll be lucky if you live another two years."

This was the medical equivalent of a drive-by shooting. Something deep in Lewis's chest was fluttering; some gawky heart-valve or scrabbled bronchus was thoroughly shocked.

2

Mercifully, autonomic instinct intervened, turning on again his beating heart and snuffling air-ways; though Lewis's mind remained in a sudden winter of deep-shock.

The doctor's pretty, uplifted face struggled to convert youthful beauty and intelligence into sombre gravitas, but Lewis thought that her softness was begging courtship and love: youth is not the stuff of unsmiling gloom and clinical efficiency.

At heart Dr Rosen was still a girl, worried about her crooked front tooth, resentful of the young mothers and her own inability to find a boyfriend who could put a coherent sentence together. Despite her cleverness and education Dr Rosen was still burdened with nature's longing for children. Motherhood, the highest function of our species, figured in all her judgements. It was the only thing that could make tears come to her eyes. The thought of not having children was the only thing that could tear her heart up.

She had nightly panics that her ovaries were being used up, her eggs wastefully harvested by her monthly cycle. She pictured her uterus in her imagination, like on a video screen, and wondered when the impatient organ would be brought to life. Dr Rosen had placed her womb on a waiting list, with the highest priority.

She couldn't help looking over men of her own age *very* closely; checking out their clear eyes, their clothes, hairstyles. She was sizing them up, looking for someone who could appreciate her, do justice to her qualities. Her disappointing appraisals constantly pulled down the corners of her mouth. Dr Rosen could unerringly put her finger on a man's pulse and feel his disloyal blood, believing that by palpating the blood she could touch the heart: find the quiddity. She could grope a guy's entire personality with a fingertip.

Dr Rosen put in long hours at the hospital, then, at home, she put in hours on the phone, vetting the supplicants from the dating agency. Hours spent listening to falsified lives. Most men she met she thought of in medical terms, the language of her trade: deficient, congenital, malignant. Some men reminded her of viruses, pathogens that invade the body and force it to make copies of themselves.

"You know, Mr Lewis, what you're doing is not only hurting yourself, it's hurting your family." The attraction that her softness had raised in him quickly turned to irritation.

"I don't have any family," he sighed. "I'm a lonely saddo. That's why I drink. Some people have religion, some have love, I have the drink. Perhaps if I'd had someone like you in my life, it might have been different. You could have made me drunk on love."

The Hippocratic heroine's face became ripe with embarrassment, her pink face hovering over her white coat like an Easter moon rising above a frostbound horizon. Her blushes formed a gauzy veil that spilled upwards from her throat.

Lewis already regretted lying to her, halving the true amount of booze he consumed. A worthless lie, as he knew they always doubled the amount given.

It was a pity that they couldn't have had a real conversation, one where each could have spoken their mind. There was nothing too nasty or shameful to be said. What Lewis couldn't tell her about, despite her Mater Dolorosa warmth, (you couldn't look into her face without thinking of the Madonna), was about a mother's death that left a child's mind locked in grey ice, about the whirlpools and vortices that convinced a boy that life was more than he could bear.

He never left the death room, never stopped being a kid gazing into his mother's coffin. Losing a parent deforms a child's soul, mutilates innocence, vandalises wonderment. Making Death's acquaintance so young turns light-heartedness into a squalid commodity. A Niagara of booze hadn't stopped the longing for affection. He still cried for her; age never made a man of Lewis.

After being severed from love like that, he was always pining to get back, looking for love, falling in love; love was always the motive. This longing for what he had lost left him with no interest in self-preservation. Lewis got the message at ten years old: that life was as prickly as a stinging nettle. He never learned how to grasp it without getting hurt.

"Then you should stop drinking for yourself, Mr Lewis. Liver failure is an unpleasant way to go. Alcohol is a very clumsy way of killing yourself."

Her voice had become pensive, more concerned, her eyes glittered with professional wisdom. There was not a trace of girlish giggle or teenage mirth about her. She was DEADLY serious. Her face was now quite pale, the colour of latte coffee. Her clean cheekbones had the smoothness of yielding ivory, making him even more self-conscious about his own lunar visage.

Lewis couldn't help loving the doctor. Like Jesus, she was dedicated to persuading people towards prudence and discretion, given to saving and redeeming the lost with inspired utterances.

But Lewis was no Lazarus, he had no unfinished human business. He was a hostage to her gentleness, her slim hands and her sea-grey eyes that gazed into the distance when she was thinking.

He tried to imagine the white-coated doctor with her eyes closed, hair undone and lying sweatily across her face, a sigh unbuckling

6

from her moist lips. His Men's Mag. image of her sucked the breath from his lungs. He wondered how often she danced, how often she drank wine in the afternoon – when did she last make love? He imagined her lying in his arms, her post-lovemaking skin breathing odours of the rain-forest, the musky, humid scent of hot-house arboretum. Lewis inhaled the nutmeg pungency of her body's own eau-de-cologne. Love would be the only thing that could reach across the chasm between them, bridge the abyss of age, class and stupefying dipsomania. The visionary John Lennon sung it in his numinous vox Dei, the absolving, intercessory: "ALL YOU NEED IS LOVE, LOVE IS ALL YOU NEED."

On the doctor's bookshelves at home you would find, among her Gray's Anatomy and other medical tomes, masses of gardening and cookery books, a few Joanna Trollopes and one or two tyranny-overcoming Catherine Cooksons. When you entered Dr Rosen's home you were convinced you were in the nest of an entirely adorable creature, whose main characteristics were meekness and decency. Lewis believed she had his share of both.

He knew that Dr Rosen's severity was for his own good – he didn't have it in him to change, but it was an excellent thing to have her care about him. How could he explain to her that his body, with its working arms and legs, its focusing eyes and fitful intelligence, and all its other perfections, was meant for a happier, more normal soul?

He could tell that Dr Rosen saw her patients holistically (a horror most doctors avoided), as individuals with their great passions and foolishness and heroism. But her appraisal of people was sourced from love, goodness and a deeply honest belief in humanity. These were her fundamental assumptions, and the reason for her doctor's vocation. What was left out of her philosophy was the fact that some people cannot swallow what life has stuffed down their throats.

In fear and uncertainty, Lewis's 'irrepressible' look was stumbling towards her. Dr Rosen was trying to save him from the sordid, inexpedient winter that lay ahead. He heard himself saying in a show-off voice:

"Oh, I don't know, I think killing yourself with booze is the perfect response to life."

She stared at him blankly, unblinking, her mouth as thin and straight as a hypodermic needle.

"It's up to you, Mr Lewis. There's nothing more I can say. You know what will happen to you."

Despite the sunlight glancing off the venetian blinds into the temperate zone of the long hospital corridor, Lewis could feel that a hard winter was coming on. Around him, in the consulting rooms spaced out like Stations of the Cross, the death-avoiders, their lives on hold, were calling in their N.H.S. warranties. Telephones were ringing, electronic devices fussed and fibrillated, egalitarian-uniformed nurses, the elite trench-fighters in the disease wars, came and went on life-or-death missions. Every cog and wheel in the vast healing machine was cranking away, straining and groaning, the accelerator flat to the floor.

Fear had infiltrated into his arms and legs. He was walking down the pale-green corridor feeling like some serial killer being hauled off to the chair, rubber-legged, moaning and screaming. But he wasn't kicking and struggling as he handed himself over for annihilation. Oh no, Lewis's was a brisk step, a jaunty stride; he was friskily running towards his oblivion like a raising-Cain terrorist, like a malignant al-Qaeda bomber.

When he got home he poured himself a millionaire measure of Scotch and helped his big liver into a chair. Raising the drink to his recidivist lips, he waited for the tell-tale steadying of the hand. Then, in a disappointing Hollywood accent, he said out loud: "You're gonna fry for this, kid."

Outside, in the anxious darkness, the crowd had fallen silent; everything had been done, everything tried. Further effort was useless. As the lights flickered, a shadowy head lowered in sympathy; a tear fell to the sizzling pavement.

10

# Colours Of The Moon

She tried to blink away the tears in her eyes, but there were too many to deal with and so she shut them tight. Someone leaned over her face and said with a voice so close that it seemed to come from inside her own head, "You OK?"

She nodded.

"I've put the money on the table."

The door to the room closed with a soft click. She opened her eyes and sat up. The man who had spoken was no longer there. Her posture suddenly relaxed.

"Come on, get up," she said wearily to herself. "It's only half-past ten."

She walked forward and picked up the neatly folded money from the table.

"Better be off."

Delving into her handbag, she found the two tabs of speed she had been saving; the drug's chemical smile and ridiculous optimism would help her to stay awake, to keep going.

She glanced down at her legs and moaned. Her poor stockings were churned and torn. She reached down to touch them, thinking: at least the flesh is whole. She was all right, that's what mattered.

Back on the street, a man came running up behind her and spun her around.

"What the fuck have you been doing up there? You've been ages," he snorted, his voice buckling with venom.

"Whad' you think I've been doin'?" she said loudly. "It took me ages to get 'im to come."

He grabbed her arm and walked her towards a shop doorway. She dragged her feet as she followed him, as though heavy lead weights had been attached to them.

The man pushed her into the deep doorway and held her slight shoulders against the curving plate glass. He shook his head several times.

"You people…"

She was looking at the floor, but she could feel his eyes boring into her face.

"Where's your sense of duty, eh?"

Where was her sense of anything? she wondered. She couldn't connect with anything; her mind went on forever but contained nothing – nothing but apologies. She turned her face up to look into the shining square eyes of the man. In those bright windows she thought she glimpsed a frightened figure. Then she realised it was her own reflection she was looking at. Is everyone scared, she wondered, or is it just me?

The man who held her shoulders took one hand away and held it ready at his side. She sensed the imminence of harm. Any second now he'd slap her. Or would he…?

– BLAM!

The puzzle was solved. Her cheek throbbed and roared, a hellish distress of flayed roots and nerves. She wondered why the painful things that happened to her seemed to pass by so slowly. A split-second slap in the face could drift by like an extruded hour. She had taken many slaps from this man. Some of them big ones.

"Give me what you've got."

She delved into her bra, and handed over the money. The man counted the notes. "Get fucking busy. You've got to make at least another two hundred tonight."

When the man had gone, she moved in the direction of the light. Abruptly, the passageway widened into a place where movement began, and new kinds of people walked, or sat at tables, or yelled and screamed spectacularly in the middle of the street.

She raised her hands to her eyes, blocking out the cool wash of air and light. Then she moved forward, carefully, to avoid the thrashing pockets of confusion and distress that littered the pavements. When she tried to accelerate down the street, the long thin stilettos on her shoes abruptly checked her. She bent down to adjust the straps. Two passing men carrying bottles of beer shouted and thrust their pelvises at her meaningfully. But she could smell the air now, and hurried away from their leprous gazes.

A top-class hotel, a few drinks, and some excellent golf on a new and challenging course. He'd been looking forward to it. When he arrived home from work on the Friday, his wife had already packed his case (including the aspirin). Now it was Saturday night and he'd enjoyed a great day of golf up at the Whitchurch club. After a juicy steak in the hotel's restaurant, he was feeling very satisfied with his life.

It was nearly midnight but, outside, the street was as busy as the bar of the Angel Hotel. He'd been given some directions by the porter, and now he eased the car forward at a walking pace; only when the crowd had thinned did he allow himself a side-ways glance through the window. Thigh-booted, mini-skirted girls walked the street, stopping occasionally to perfume the shadows of doorways, peering out like sybaritic snipers. Their luminous faces, masked by orange neon, seemed to scold him. They had a signal look, betraying contempt and easy availability. Easy: though not necessarily cheap.

His breath tasted metallic and smelled faintly of whisky. His hands sweated and trembled as he gripped the steering wheel.

14

"What do you do?" he asked himself. "How the hell does this work?"

Instinctively he wanted to do the right thing, observe the etiquette; he'd never done anything like this before and he was desperate to avoid making a complete fool of himself. He felt like a new boy at school, a school with sordid rules and unseen dangers. He remembered how much he'd hated school, with its tribalised bullying and humiliations. Now he wondered who did the bullying and degrading here, on the contentious, newspaper-blown streets – the pimps, the cops, poverty and exclusion, or men like him?

He U-turned at the top of the road and stopped the car. His head slumped against his hands resting on the wheel and a long, drawn out sigh whistled across his lips like pressure being released from a steam-engine.

"I only want to see what it's like," he said. "I just want to see how it feels."

It was an honest answer to an unasked question. After a decade of being married to Judy, he'd begun to look at other women and wondered what it would be like to make love with them. For him, it was the Twelve Year Itch, a variation on the wantonly filmic Seven Year Itch. He couldn't help it. It was like looking in a shop window and coveting the things he saw there – window shopping, he called it. That's all it was.

For a second it struck him that he was the last person he'd expect to see here. He still had a deep-seated love for Judy; their lives had melted into one, become smoothly interlocked like a silken zipper. They had grown up together, sweethearts, then engagement, then the expected marriage. Their worlds had always turned on the same axis. But now, after twelve years of observing the marital rules, more than a decade of bright-eyed uxoriousness, he was sitting here, looking for a lace-trimmed whore among these working girls, with their ice-cube-hard stares and quid pro quo smiles.

There had never been anyone but Judy and he was afraid he'd missed out on something, afraid that something exciting had passed him by. He had to know. He had to find out what sex with a different woman was like. He slid the window down, letting in a rush of cold air. A wave of self-loathing tumbled in with the smell of car exhaust, squeezing at the back of his throat. A long groan twisted his lips and face into a grimace of pained frustration. An erection was already declaring itself, nudging aside his boxers and resting its thermodynamic heaviness on his thigh.

The smiling face of his wife loomed into his consciousness. He couldn't help thinking that lately she looked the part of the weary, put-upon mother and wife. Although she had only just reached forty, the march of the years and two small, demanding children had left their brushstrokes upon her. Her face, once as clear as a windblown sky, was now clouded with a network of lines and a string-bag of leaking veins.

So why, he wondered, when he was thinking about betraying his wife, did he suddenly think of his children? Why now, when he should have been able to occlude them in the blinding radiation of his lust? Why did their sleeping faces come humming into his porn-served consciousness? Their innocent sweetness converged on the pit of him, threatening to tear him inside out.

"You OK?" The female voice startled him. He turned. She had her hand on the half-opened window. Her p.v.c. coat glowed like tin-foil, momentarily huge and artificial, as if some hulking pyramid faced with tiny mirrors had attached itself to his car. Her face loomed, smiling and magical, flayed by the shadowy light into diffuse strips of parchment. She was young. Very young.

"You OK?" she asked again. He nodded, apologetically. The girl's bony face was thin and a little masculine; there was no real femininity in her features. Her beauty lay in her eyes, clever, adolescent eyes that threw fistfuls of sorcerous light into the idling car. The light from her eyes scared him. Like Aladdin lamps, they gleamed hidden promise, scooping him up and drawing him in.

"Shall I get in?" she asked. Her eyebrows had risen to meet her hair-line. She was nodding encouragement.

"But…" he began to say. It was too late; she was already sat next to him, eagerly straightening out the helter-skelter plastic of her crackling raincoat. She looked him up and down, assessing the possible threat, the likelihood of a mugging or worse. His neat blazer and wide-eyed anxiety reassured her.

"You want to go to my place or do you have somewhere to go?"

He thought of all the problems of taking her back to his hotel: the porter's knowing smile and the sniffy looks from the late night drinkers in the bar he'd have to pass through to get to the lifts; not to mention the possibility of bumping into his golfing friends.

"No… Your place is fine."

"So what's your name?" she asked, as he drove off.

"Sevy," he replied. "Sevy Nicklaus."

The girl remained silent. He thought he'd got away with it. Then:

"Hey," she laughed. "You should've been a golfer with a name like that."

He glanced across at the two swellings beneath the girl's low-cut top and tried to imagine himself suckling at her erect nipples. Judy's nipples never got that hard anymore, they were inverted and temperamental; sometimes they were impossible to get erect

18

enough to flick with his tongue. He supposed that they were now just the workaday milk-teats of a wife and mother, atrophied appendages that had been too-long gummed and twanged by two hungry babies and one nipple-fixated husband.

"How old are you?" he asked. "Do your parents know what you get up to?"

"My parents are dead." More out of desire to change the subject than indignation, she added, "Don't talk to me about my parents."

She was stretched out on a rug among the ferns, lying side-by-side with a man she loved, naked, kissing and touching his body. She kissed the palms of his hands and then his wrists, all the while gazing up at the flush of pride in his wide and grateful eyes. Then she pulled his face down to her breasts, moaning as he flicked her budding nipples with his tongue. She lay wrapped in his arms in the bower of ferns, amid the soft murmurings of a river and the summer-scented air. She was thinking, his body – my body, where's the difference? Where's the join?

It's hard to convey, to describe, how emblematically love sits on the consciousness of someone who has never been in love, but this was her escape. When she lay down with her tricks, she would escape to love. She was a sop for love; soaking up its rescuing exemptions, syphoning to the dregs its cheerful protectiveness. She thought that she should be able to spray love over herself like a perfume, its gaseous haze dulling the edge of pain, soothing the noxious day-to-day scatology that sought her out. She blessed hard-working Cupid; his toil aerated her soul.

All men looked alike to her. But to say that all men looked alike was like saying that all men's teeth were alike. The reason that they all looked alike was because she thought they all wanted to eat her, to consume her body. They just want to eat me, that's all, she thought. The pandemonium of men she met, with their swollen bellies and cocks, their fierce eyes and their barbed-wire legs, their slyness and athleticism, their frantic breathing and writhing – they all looked alike to her.

One day, in the street, she had seen a smartly dressed young man gazing at her. He was looking at her with patient, serious eyes. She remembered those eyes, and liked to think about them. Such thoughtful eyes. Perhaps, she hoped, one day, all men would look at her like that.

Now the man with the car had gone and she was lying on the rumpled bed, thinking about her relationship with her father. It had been formed out of commonality of interest. They had formed an Electra alliance against a common enemy: her mother.

At home she had witnessed some terrible fights. Her mother used to start off berating her

Dad for all the things he did that annoyed her, then, little by little, she'd turn her vituperative tongue on her daughter, and start going on about all the things she did to get on her nerves. She hated her mother, and her father hated his cruel, bullying wife; her favoured form of communication was throwing a cup at her husband's head.

And then, one day, her father had confronted her mother with the rumour of her infidelity. The next day she came home from school and – poof! Her mother was gone. She'd cleaned out the house, taking everything, including the television and video. A few months later her mother went to court and hammered her Dad on the ancillary settlement, taking the house and a slice of his pension. Her Dad had disappeared over the horizon, and, within a year, her mother had put her into council care.

The next morning, back in the tiled brightness of his hotel bathroom, he found he couldn't shave. Every time he tried to look into the mirror he had to turn away. He couldn't look at himself. He doubted he could ever look at himself again. He shaved himself like a blind man, staring blankly at the wall. His heart felt as though it had been pounced upon by a lion; it felt flattened and torn.

Fear gripped his whole body; it was as though some inky impress marked him with treachery, a dark wine-stain dissembled his face. He knew he wore his secret like a flag as big as half the sky. His children's faces momentarily rose in his mind's eye, then faded, bleached in dismay. Now he knew, he knew what having another woman felt like. It felt like an earthquake, a tectonic shift that had ripped through his life, leaving a chasm between him and his wife and his kids.

He wanted to call home, but he knew he'd just blubber his confession down the phone. He could never tell her, which made him doubly guilty; he'd have to conceal this immense thing from her forever, paring away at his soul like an axe. He cursed himself silently and sat slumped on the edge of the bath, slowly shaking his head from side to side.

"I must have been mad, out of my stupid, stupid mind." He wanted to be allowed to put back his life to where it had been, but he knew it had already begun to decompose. Fidelity, restfulness, spontaneity – ended, cracked open, admitting the ugliness of lies. His life was a hostage, hanging by a fraying thread of deceit.

"I should have just kept my mind on the golf."

He leaned his aching head against the porcelain of the hand-basin, the cold penetrating the panicked clockwork of his mind. He might as well have gone home and demolished their house, scattered their belongings and left. It felt like he had abandoned the ones he loved, like he was lost in space, the earth a remote blue spot falling away. He felt lonely and vulnerable, like a forgotten child. He wished he'd given his kids one more hug, one more kiss before he'd left home.

Now he felt he could never go home; nothing would ever be simple again. From this day on he could never be exactly himself; he would be crouched guiltily within his shabby shell, trapped in his shame like a mosquito in amber. He felt his whole body trembling around his culpable, self-destructive heart.

\* \* \*

The cocaine lay on its opened foil, coolly waiting for her, ready to open its doors and well aware of its obsessive power, its bewildering ability to subdue loitering phantoms. The Blow was a yellow-creamy colour, its powdered granules lumped together into a tiny cairn. It looked good. Taking out a razor blade, she chopped herself a couple of lines, rolled a straw in her fingers, and then snorted the lines up. "Mmm…" She hadn't made enough money for her pimp, and she knew what that meant. She knew that a thing like this would happen to her sometime.

Running its electric currents across her forebrain, the coke quickly began its anaesthetic crunch, cleaning and polishing the hot thudding pockets of reality from her mind

23

like a neurological steam-jet. Reality – the rendezvous of mind and matter – quickly became tractable, merely a coherent delusion providing fodder for her fantasies, technicolour screenplays for her dreams. The drug allowed her to cancel out the testimony of the senses, sedating the day's disasters. A delusion of well-being was moving rapidly across the scrimmages of synapses in her cerebral-cortex, making life beautiful, ethereal, new-born.

After switching off the light, she lay down on the bed again, in the still-warm impress where two bodies had just lain. Looking out of the window she saw an extremely lovely creature. A fat sleepy thing hovered and basked. She saw an imperial moon, hanging on a backdrop of purple calm.

The yellow energy hurt her eyes, so she lowered her gaze to the tufted outline and crenellations of the city's silhouette. The steep canyons of the streets boiled with rage, humiliation and fear. The high glass walls of office blocks bruised the distance, warping perspectives and making everything seem nearer.

Where was she going to hide? There was always too much light buzzing and arcing, not enough shadows, not enough darkness to hide. It was then that her sense of danger started to rise sharply. Soon someone would come and do her damage.

"Enough of this," she thought. "Do it!"

She was running. She was running as though she had somewhere to go. Egged on by fear, running pleased her. The city was moving past her at quite a speed. Sombre bricks and sparkling glass reeled by. She seemed to be able to run as fast as she liked. She thought that running would save her, take her to some place where there were no people to hurt her. The concrete pavement spun past, spanning out into another life, a different life to the one she was in.

Overhead she noticed that the fat moon was heavy and red now. Still she moved forward, bent at the waist, arms pumping, running as fast as she could. With a lurching breath, she finally fell exhausted on to a grass verge. Her body began to spasm and quiver as she fought for breath. This is it, she thought, this is how it ends.

She tried to roll over on to her back, but the movement was painful and it took her quite a long time. Her body was damp with sweat but her mouth was completely dry. Her body was always getting things wrong like that. Poor body, she thought. Sad, that's what it is. My body is sad. And it's melting away. She lay for a while and listened to her thoughts. The words of her thoughts were not forming properly, but they managed to say a lot about sadness, and confusion, and absent fathers, and uncaring mothers. Then she stopped listening to her thoughts, and waited.

From where she lay, she could see the heroic poem of the sky unfolding, the clouds shuddering in the wind, the stars falling like confetti, the moon a corpulent bee flying through the haze. All this she saw in the voluptuous dome through painful and ragged eyes.

She wondered whether the moon was ever afraid, living its life, as it did, as another life's reflection, its mirror, its shadow. She thought that the moon's changing light was revealing something to her, or would soon reveal something, or had already revealed something that she had missed and would never see again.

Around her stilled form, she heard the shouts and vibrations of the night, the snorting traffic, the slammed car doors, the breathing of machines. She could hear the sizzling of the night all along the long defile of Manor Way.

Her heart started missing its beat, halting and stuttering, its corpuscular bales of blood gumming in her arteries. From deep within her, violent convulsions squeezed unwanted sounds through her lips. She was crying and whimpering. She told herself to be quiet. What was the point of hiding if she made all that noise? As she was telling herself to be good, she noticed something different about her breath. Usually she could feel her breath hunching and pressing. Now it wasn't. It felt like her breath had abandoned her, discarded her, resigned. High above her, the frightened moon went out, and the blackness in the raw and quivering sky came swooping down. Her eyes were still open, but they said nothing.

Behind the grassy bank on which her body lay, the smoothed and manicured lawns of Whitchurch Golf Club breathed the earth's viridian breath, and slept their pampered sleep, dreaming their triumphal dreams of laureled hole-in-one glory. The creeping weight of night-time dew moved past her up the bank with pitying timidity, and dropped its soft tears on the eighteenth green. The sorrowful dew could see the stark facts of the scene, and couldn't understand it: couldn't understand its inordinateness, its callous misogyny, its fierce inhumanity. The dew lingered with brimming eyes and curled an arm around the lifeless girl: it knew that even the loss of a child means nothing if there's no one there to feel it.

# Fanatics

First, my State of Mind…

I admit I'm no Western Mail political Journo, and there are many things I have never understood, but it appears to me there's been a savage polarisation in this town: an economic 'Wall' has been thrown up along the east bank of the TAFF, and I for one want to know what the fuck is going on.

I suspect that the sack-of-dead-rats who govern us began by drawing a line down the middle of the river; French fries, Fat Cat business operations and expense accounts this side, chips and underworld drug-madness the other.

The pro-development money-suckers have grabbed every chunk of land for their hubristic, space-killing buildings that nobody but the tourists give a fuck about – I was too stoned to make it to the polls last time, so there's no point in screaming at the Power Whores in the street, but next election, I'm going to vote those dead-beat greed-head jackals the fuck out of there.

I've just remembered what Dylan said about all those poll-watching Politicos, (no, I don't mean THAT Dylan, I mean Dylan THE POET).

"...Don't follow leaders and watch the parkin' meters."

You know, sometimes I think that poor old Dylan (Thomas) has got it easy. He's only dead – I'm STILL struggling to make a living out of writing.

...And fuck the tourists, let them look up at the mountains.


It's past midnight on the WRONG side of town and I've drunk enough Bow and ingested enough chemicals to give me the balls to tell you Portnoys what the score is around here. I'm giving you a snapshot of my days and nights living in the Pressure Cooker; the edgy side of the city that most people don't see.

You know, some people get nervous just driving through our estate. But I'm a FREAK myself and I can take living in the TOO MUCH FUN CLUB; all the drugs and violence and joy and only parking under street-lights. It's brutal living in the slaughter-house, and I love it.

Because it's here that the Rimbaud Spirit survives among the Wobblies and Weirdos, the dope-heads and attack-dogs. It's here that us first-person stream-of-consciousness scribblers pretend that reality is fiction and lefty Red Poets and Anarchists and Full-Moon Revolutionaries plot vengeance against the SYSTEM.

It's here that doomed shave-headed kids fight with the cops and smoke marijuana pipes and drive around looking for stray dogs to run over, or slam stolen cars at 100 mph into innocent trees.

And they don't know why they've been crushed and beaten and stabbed in the back by political geeks. But they know that NOBODY can rescue them.

All these things are happening right here, right now…

And you wonder why we look at you strangely?

\* \* \*

To:Prisoner 01336702
Remand Wing Cardiff Gaol

Hey, Scumbag!
You should have been locked up a long time ago – you are truly beyond redemption. I hope you're enjoying the vortex-madness down at the Sad Hotel! And how's the close contact with all those aggressively naked men every night? Watch out for Big Bob in the showers and for fuck's sake don't tell them about your interest in antique china!

Maria told me she's afraid that when you get out you're going to be into some strange lusts, but I told her not to worry, it's HER job to get you into sick-bastard sex. (By the way, she's beautiful when she walks around naked, and so am I. We've enclosed a photograph.)

Anyway, we all miss you. You're a preternatural Warrior, Ginger, you could have ridden with Ghengis or rowed with the Vikings; you always had a fine eye for a fight – you nasty little bugger. Being your friend is like diving into a pool that got emptied yesterday; there's always pain, but there's always FUN, with a silent scream in the throat. But so what? You are a necessary PAIN IN THE ARSE.

You are also RIGHT, Ginger – it does take a LOT of love to love Freedom. And what better *Casus Belli* than the Fanatics trying to take over? The time has come to kick some ass – what if they won! We'd all be wearing burkas and beating ourselves with whips and crawling on our hands and knees in penance to Fuck-knows-where. Though let's face it, on the scale of religious fanaticism, those guys you malleted from God Inc. are fucking dwarfs. And you've got to be a Vigilante Joke or a dunce to start turning them into sausage-meat just for interrupting the Game. So let's leave Tony and the bozo-rich-kid-President to sort the FANATICS out, shall we?

Nobody needs your hyperkinetic arse in jail, my friend, especially when the Season starts. We've ALL got better things to do than visit you up Shit Creek. You're a good man, Ginger, but Jesus, let's at least wait for the FREAKS to burn our flag before we make war on the Mothers. (There's a thin line between healthy antagonism and the Manson Family.) Oh, what the hell, we're a free people, and freedom is an amazing thing: so let's shit on the chests of the Fanatics – they've got BAD ideas.

Anyway, don't get crazy, don't get queer, and get BACK on the fucking street.

Live Free Or Die, My Man.
CLANG!

Now let's get one thing straight, Ginger is the most spiritual person I know – except perhaps for that Jesus freak who used to walk around town scaring the holy shit out of everyone with a board that said THE WORLD IS ABOUT TO END. (If he really believed that, how come he was walking around with a stupid sign instead of abandoning himself to piss-ups and orgies? Hey?)

Anyway, Ginger is the most spiritual person I know, and I don't mean in the mainstream religious sense; he enjoys the company of Druids, Shamans, assorted Witches and even the occasional Witness, if she's pretty enough

33

and enjoys a glass or two of booze to help oil the machinery of mystical speculation.

There's something else ye of little faith should know – I secretly worship the *Creator Spiritus* myself; mainly because He (or She!) leaves me the fuck alone. So, the point is, it isn't like me and Ginge are a couple of Antichrists or anything. Which makes what happened that Saturday afternoon even more weird.

It was a cold, foggy afternoon in January, and it was the Wales vs. England rugby match. (How come the nation only gets an adult dose of patriotism when we play the Sais – The Old Enemy?) We hadn't beaten the bastards since Methuselah played for Judea's under-fifteens. My girlfriend had gone shopping with her sister and Ginger was coming around with a case of Bow. I'd already opened a half of Scotch and rolled a few sticks of Blue Mountain weed. We had all we needed for a very relaxing afternoon – win or lose.

Let me say right here that Ginge isn't an animal, in fact he's quite domesticated. He knows how to get drunk and stoned without causing a scene or acting like some junk-fiend shit-head. Ginge knows how to handle himself in polite company; that's what made what happened even more confusing.

It was just after the start of the second half when there was a knock at the door. At first I ignored it. Then I made a BIG mistake: I decided to see who had the bare-arsed nerve to come around when THE match was on. When I opened the door I couldn't believe my poor blood-shot eyes. Standing right there on my Saturday afternoon doorstep were two of Salt Lake City's finest: the Mormons had come to town – and they were on a suicide mission.

Now, there's something you may not know about me, and that's my interest in cosmology, which gives me a pretty good understanding of what IS possible and what is NOT possible in this bottomless pit of a universe. I think we can agree, that religion is all about what is NOT possible. And so I was thinking, as I stood shivering on that cold door-step gazing into two stupidly frozen smiles: "This is NOT FUCKING POSSIBLE!" Didn't these morons know there was a game on?

The pair mumbled something about being Todd and Tad, or Tim and Flick or some other bullshit nonsense. (Jeezus, I hate those Holleewood accents.) Their right hands were thrust in my direction, ready to shake. I just stood there, dumbfounded. "What the fuck!" was all I could mumble.

Then I heard Ginger stomping down the hall behind me. "They've gone too fucking far this time!" he bellowed. He was madder than a bag full of snakes.

"There goes the game," I thought.

"Hi folks, my name is Ginger."

"Hi, Ginger, how are you." Two right hands shot out in Ginge's direction, followed up with the, "I'm Hubba" and "I'm Bubba" routine.

"I've got a question for you guys," Ginger said, silkily. "And I want you to think carefully before you answer – 'cos this one is BIG. This is the one you'll have to answer when you come face to face with GOD ALMIGHTY!"

The two proselytes looked bewildered, like rabbits caught in a headlight that was barrelling down on them. "HE will ask you: 'What was your greatest SIN? Speak up now, boys, or I'll send you straight to Hell…' What will you say, boys? And remember, HE will judge you." The Mormons just stared at Ginger, speechless and filling up fast with animal fear and un-Christian malice. Then Ginge let rip.

"WHAT in the name of God's shit are you playing at?" he screamed at them. "What kind of dangerous fucking MANIACS come to talk God when there's a fucking Game on? THIS is your greatest SIN!"

What comes next is horrible, as vicious as an acid flashback…But remember, in the right circumstances, we are all SWINE and WEIRDOS and BABBLING STRANGERS. So…it was just another Crazy Fucked-up afternoon. Right?

I don't know exactly what triggered the shit storm; maybe somebody blinked. I heard a faint click as Ginger's fist connected at warp-speed with the tallest guy's nose. It started raining blood; bright red droplets of pain began to hit the door-step. Jesus, those All-American noses can bleed.

Then the other bloke had Ginge in a headlock, trying to wrestle him to the ground. I didn't bother to help, Ginge didn't need any. He shook the Mormon off, and then I heard a click as another Yankee schnozzle succumbed to a well-placed head-butt. The Mormons ran off up the road, whimpering something about THE LAW.

"Go tell the Ayatollahs!" Ginger was yelling after them.

"Shit, Ginge, we're DOOMED. Those Suckers will call out the Armed Response Gang for this. We're gonna DIE you mad Fuck!"

"Fear no evil, my friend. God is with us on this one."

I admit, ganja paranoia was kicking in. I was panicking; red dots all along a grey pavement is a sickening sight. It looked like some ghoulish *Pointilliste* had gone ape-shit with a can of red paint. OK, re-telling the story now, I can see that it was all pretty sickening.

About twenty minutes later, there was another knock at the door.

"Those stupid bastards are back!" yelled Ginger, charging like a bonzai rhino for the front door.

"Hey lads, how's your sex life? Do you two hold hands in bed?"

37

I thought Ginger was just abusing the Mormons again.

"We've had a very serious complaint, sir. It's about a couple of assaults."

The Enemy rolled right over us that cold, January afternoon. Ginger got three months for that one. It was a BAD business. Although, outside the court, one of the cops said he thought my friend was a hero. I'll never forget Ginge's reply when the judge finished his summing up:

"What are you talking about? What crime? Where's the fucking CRIME?"

Indeedy, my Dopehead Don-Keh-Ho-Tee. Indeedy.

You'll be happy to hear that they turned Ginger out after six weeks of porridge: something to do with good behaviour. (Uh!) I met him outside the Gate with a half-bottle of Jack Daniels and a spliff like a pit-prop. As we walked to the pub I asked him:

"So, did you do a lot of abstract political thinking in there? You know, the 21st Century American Imperialism thing? That usually keeps you entertained."

"No…" he replied flatly. "…I wanked a lot."

He walked along with his hands punched into his pockets, his head down to avoid the scurfing wind that escaped from the monied clutches of Yuppyville Bay. He was as pale as putty; he looked faded, out-of-focus. He looked like the lead singer of REM.

"Where the fuck's Maria?" He was frowning as he asked.

"I haven't seen her for a while," I lied.

"And I didn't like your joke about her walking around naked," he snarled.

I didn't say anything. I just saw myself standing in a long line of Judases. But I wasn't prepared to play the role of a Brutus too. Not today, of all days.

"et tu Mother-Fucker?" – BOOM.

Maybe I'll NEVER tell him; after all, Ginger's my mate, my Main Man... and he's just too SCARY to Fuck with. I hope, Grace a Dieu, Maria will remember that – YOU listening up there, Big Guy?

Of course the Booze and Drug thing is an indulgent cop-out for any really serious dispute with Life and the HUMAN RACE. But what the Fuck...I have a fondness for the simplistic.

Finally, you may find it amusing to hear that Ginge once accused me of taking myself too seriously. He reckoned that I'd probably end up choking myself with my OWN hands. My psycho psycho-analytical friend told me that I should try laughing at myself more. (He's not content with screwing his own life, he wants to metastasize his dopehead-philosophy into mine!)

But, of course, I told him that laughing at myself sounded like a neat trick and that I might try it. Why not? Everyone else seems to be laughing themselves fucking stupid around here. (During one of my visits to the genito-urinary clinic, I once made the mistake of saying that 'laughter was the best medicine'. They instantly assured me that penicillin, tetracycline and sulfa drugs beat the shit out of laughter!)

So, what the Hell...*ne cede malis*, eh?

Christ, I shudder every time I see those brooding words in print.

That's my epitaph

# The Cupboard Wife

The houses of the inexplicably rich grin and
shiver. In the long drive, Mercedes number
plates advertise Amy and Rod. Then we're lost
among the canapés and numismatic chat. We're
in the suburb of Llandaff, where the sun always
shines – this is Cardiff's Cricklewood, the
capital's stockbroker-belt. We're at Stephen's
boss's house for 'Yuletide drinks'. (Think art-
deco antiques, Persian carpets, *snobbisme* –
especially the *snobbisme.)*

I am doing my duty by my husband, though
this kind of duty is not an inexhaustible
commodity. I feel tiny among glowering giants.
All the 'higher ups' in the bank are here.
Interest rates and capital gains hang in the air
like bunting. The conversation already mauls to
and fro; but they are not for me, nor I for them.

*"Jamie's at Oxford already? But he's only
sixteen."*

It's understood that for the rich, time and
gravity are hidden.

Our two sons, the twins, are away at their own minor college, enjoying the chaotic and weightless life of students living away from home. We struggle to send them the money they swear they need. Money for fares, for running shoes, for beer and kitchen chairs; money for girls and money to learn to live with strangers.

All the women's faces are shining and merge in this enchanted realm of mirrors and chandeliers, of tennis courts and swimming pools, of surgically enhanced breasts and the power-tourney of sexual favour. These women are like musical notes on the staves of their husbands' careers. They are the hollow thumps and whining tremolos, never satisfied with the going melody, always wanting more *fortissimo*; fluttering their eyelashes until their man is playing the loudest instrument in the orchestra. The women circle the men like boxers, sizing them up, waiting for the opportunity for a discreet clinch, or a nipple-tingling maul.

Stephen's boss, as big as God, plays at goodness and mercy. (Stephen's boss playing at God is one of our 'in' jokes. His boss has never had a metaphysical thought in his life; though being rich must make being materialistic and greedy easier to bear, if you know what I mean.) He's got the winter-tanned look of a Senior golf professional who's moved on to something bigger. His gold Rolex is so huge it's impossible to ignore.

No-one troubles to talk to me, but I don't blame Stephen; his years of being insect-life at the bank were excruciating for him. Now he sips malt whisky with his boss, preening himself at approaching the summit of his career's Everest: promotion to manager, his own branch in Whitchurch.

He nods and smiles at every sentence his boss utters, sipping his drink each time his boss does and forgetting about his creeping deafness. He can hear everything when it suits him and, tonight, it definitely suits him. I'm left standing alone, frozen with forgotten names and unfamiliar faces.

It strikes me how nicely ironic it is that Stephen and I met at a socialist student dance in college; Stephen, a bloody Socialist! Christ, how often I've thought that he needs re-acquainting with ideals more fundamental than the Financial Times Share Index.

He was reading Geography and I was studying Physics. How the hell did he get into banking with a geography degree and why, when he started in the bank, did he suddenly decide to become the village White Capitalist Pig?

I gave up any thoughts of a career when I fell pregnant with the twins. I thought at the time that I would prefer to play the mousey-haired housewife, the fatigued and sweaty mother.

Back then, raising the kids seemed more important than watching Newtonian balls running down an inclined plane. Boy, was THAT a mistaken career choice! Before the boys left, we struggled to find enough space in the house; now we could have a lodger and no one would notice. The place feels like a terrestrial Black Hole.

Stephen has told me that his boss has a few drinks before his guests arrive, just to steady his nerves. Then he drinks all evening and, when the guests leave, has several night-caps to wind down. Like all true alcoholics, he has no idea how much he drinks, often wondering what happened to that last case of Scotch; "Winnie, who the hell has been drinking my best whisky? Get on the phone to the off-licence. Tell them it's an emergency." Stephen's boss can drink like Americans can eat.

Apparently, Winnie isn't too concerned about her husband's over-the-top drinking. It keeps him out of her bed and usually out of the house. Stephen's boss is a respected denizen of the local golf club: the Regional Bank Manager constantly sucked up to by the local businessmen. On most Wednesday afternoons, Winnie enjoys a bit of sucking up herself, with her young gardener.

As soon as he gets into our bed later tonight, Stephen will instantly turn away from me and dream his dreams of having his own office and his very own secretary to water his windowsill shrubs and flowers.

Now, in a dusty gulch of the drying-up conversation with his boss, he purses his lips and then touches them with his index finger, faking thoughtfulness, pretending he is considering all that has just been said. Sometimes I find it hard to believe that I ever loved this man, that I ever wanted to touch every part of him with my hands, tongue, lips. Although love has retreated, he still takes it for granted. Of course, when I was young I thought that the world was infinitely supplied with romance and that I would be a grateful life-time recipient of it. I was very young, not yet nineteen, and despite reading Physics, I was ignorant of natural law.

I have a photograph in a drawer at home. It's of Stephen and me on our first holiday; we're posing, half-naked on a beach in Spain. I was a beautiful teenager: sleek black hair, tiny waist and breasts high up on my chest with small pink nipples. Almost twenty-three years later, I can't help crying every time I pick up the damn thing.

I wonder what these lives, wasted on money, do for guidance and delight? With all this wealth involved, is love as insoluble, as unreachable for them? Is all this just a brilliantly contrived window display, a mock up? If I were to insert myself into any of these marriages, would I feel married at all? Would I feel the tremor of fear these women feel whenever a new 'girlfriend' appears on the scene? An affair for these priapic power-brokers is just pure entertainment: it has all the emotional significance of going to the pictures. Extra-marital sex, for them, is right up there with *Star Wars* and *Lord of the Rings*.

All those interminable affairs, the tearful confessions and carefully balanced martyrdoms. These women would prefer exploding coffee-cups and silent stares to divorce. When the scales are this loaded, divorce is never an option. So their marriages have been dismantled like the parts of old cars into cynical separateness. But these women haven't learned a thing about tolerance, they have simply learned the perfect agony of loneliness inside a marriage.

This place smells so much of money it turns my stomach – a heady aroma of privileged living and leisured wealth. It's obvious: the money that lives here has been in residence for generations.

These people have never felt the cold breath of misfortune – felt it grey their hair and crack their faces. I bet these people have never, in their entire lives, waited for a bus that didn't turn up. How often have they cried in the stinging rain pushing two nappy-shitting babies home from the shops, the double-buggy laden down with groceries, human excrement and deranged wailing? They'd rather ride up the high street on an eighteen-hand hunter – a froth of tweed and silk scarves tied at the neck – hunting down a terrified animal that is a million times more in touch with the universe than they are. I can imagine some of these vegetarian scarecrows watching their pack of dogs taking huge and bloody bites out of the back of an exhausted fox.

It's hard to believe that these taciturn men, watching the women like closet Lotharios, are of the hirsute, beach-bunny, dah-do-ron-ron sixties-generation. Here they stand to attention, like woollen-suited wardrobes, stomachs sucked in, buttocks clenched, the unlikely foundations of the country's financial structure.

I used to think that people who had this kind of money understood something about life that I didn't, that they had solved some kind of mystery, answered an important question that I couldn't even think of. But now I feel I could kick these first-class, tuxedo-ed geeks in the balls for no good reason at all. I'll never see this through to midnight, not in this maddening jewellery-box.

A man in his mid-seventies stands with his desiccated wife beside me. They have been married for so long that they are incapable of having a conversation with each other, so the man is ferociously smoking a smelly cigar like a train chuffing up a steep incline. I try peering at him with disdain, but he disregards me. For these people, disregarding others must be a natural force, as unremarkable as the sun traversing the sky. The only eyes that alight on me belong to a portly Asian man, whose gold-trimmed sari-ed wife turns him away with practised efficiency, her many gold bracelets jangling like a skeleton's bones.

Seeing Stephen in this swaggering milieu, a cut-priced favourite among the glacial wives, topples something inside me. Randy for a whiff of a smile they crowd him. Jealousy closes over me like the wings of a fallen angel. That's it, I've had enough!

A cold-eyed vixen takes her husband's hand and leads him home, to a mortgaged semi with tired roof and whistling windows. Home, where he leaves me daily, feeling as frail as cut grass, as useless as a broken mirror.

# The Fevered Hive

A week ago, rockets leapt into the city night, the self-absorbed expression of a new beginning. New Year's Eve played its filigreed hand into the crystal skies. We mums and dads, aunts and uncles, shuffled from our chairs with a yawn and sang to unattended ansaphones in self-pitying soundtrack tones: *Should old acquaintance be forgot*... wishing our tattooed, socialising offspring an accusatory 'Happy New Year'. How come we parents can deliver our kids a 'Happy New Year' like stabbing them in the thigh with a biro? Some people say it's an expression of repressed rage; anger at our own spent youth.

Now, a week into the New Year, the subdued but impressively blocky Castle sits there, frost dusted, neon-lit and decorative, like a set from a Harry Potter movie. Magical, winged serpents are easily imagined, thronging the night sky above St Mary Street, attacking the chatting, pavement-pounding clubbers as they throng the taxi ranks. The dragons pursue the kids in an ecstasy of vulturing obeisances; the fierce blood-dripping fangs of lunatics and homicidal nutters are ready to tear them to pieces – BOOM!

Our sons and daughters, gathered on the street's shiny, mahogany-like high table, are offered up to the Saturday night fedayeen.

We were solid asleep, like two of those dogs that sleep forever on the tombs of medieval knights. Then the phone rang. This alone explains why what was said seemed so inauthentic; I couldn't believe what I was hearing. "A knife…into her throat." In fairness to the police, within ten minutes cars started to arrive at our house; they seemed to come from the four corners of the earth.

We sat back in the heaving police-car, the circlets of blue-flashes liquefying us with fear and vulnerability. The miracle of our marriage, the justification of her mother's loosened tummy and distended brown nipples, the shrine of all our worship, lay on some steel-cold hospital trolley, her life-blood draining away.

I opened my arms wide inside the rushing car, so as to grab as much of my girl as I could. Perhaps she was already breaking away, ascending to her heaven. I clung desperately to her lopsided smile, the memory of her child's virtue. I could feel her proximity, the bustle of her soul. I could see her sitting next to me, cross legged, her hands cupped over her knees.

She was out of body, out of this world; this was her farewell, her timorous approach at saying goodbye. Pale, blonde, wide-eyed: the image of the beautiful daughter. Gone the gangling limbs, the explosive temper of perverse scudding-cloud adolescence. I saw her with the terrible acuity of the mendicant, the outstretched hand to any redeeming deity, God or gods, fate or Fates, placebos or medication – I just wanted my little girl back.

GIVE ME BACK MY DAUGHTER YOU MURDEROUS FUCKERS.

"You don't understand. It's our DAUGHTER!" my wife was wailing. She was trembling from head to toe, vibrating like a struck tuning fork.

"She's in theatre now. She's in good hands. You will see her as soon as it's possible." The nurse's voice sliced through the air like a scalpel. She was displaying the institutional arousal that in health professionals passes for understanding.

In this encrypted terrain – the utter flatness of colour, the sickliness of the air, the very light itself – everything looked feverish, welled up and sutured. Knots of people sat in the corridor, perching on the plastic-covered seats like subdued long-tailed lemurs. An alarm seemed to be constantly going off in my head.

My wife was still boring away at the cadaverous, grotesquely tall nurse, still trying to gain us entrance to the theatres. The icon of the caring nurse seemed to be an outdated cultural phenomenon. I had neither the strength nor inclination to mix it with this creepy caricature of a carer. Tired of hammering at her for admission, my wife's beseeching tears had begun. The nurse attempted to give her a wan smile, as thin as a sliver of bone-china, freighted with contempt.

"I repeat. You will see your daughter when the doctor says it's possible."

She professed – blithely and artlessly – to have no idea when that would be.

Eventually, we were left with staring out of the sad, dead eyes of the hospital windows, gnawing at our nails and trying to flush away some of the spiralling desolation.

Up here, on the sixth floor, I surveyed the Heath's deconstruction. There used to be only one massive tower block. It stood alone, like some lumpy concrete cartilage had been dumped among the surrounding streets. Now the hospital had sucked up all the streets and snared their residents in an even more secure grid of relationship.

My wife came out of the toilet and hovered silently at my elbow. There was nothing she could possibly say…and yet…and yet…

We patted each others' arms gently as the long hours came and went.

At home, aunts and uncles were coiling up fairy lights and taking down shimmering paper, pulling small glass trinkets from the worry-soaked branches of a tree. A knocked-over mug of tea set everyone into a hair-triggered argument, then desultory moodiness. The minor accident drew interminable whys and wherefores. Everyone's ears hummed as though an explosion had just occurred.

From the corridor outside our waiting room came some jolly banter. What sounded like an acne-scarred voice was trilling, "The guy was bloody huge. Had to nut the fucker to get 'im off me." I shivered at the thought of the routine violence out there on the murky streets.

I turned to my wife. "Call home again. Better give them another update."

She reached into her bag and pulled out her mobile. She was soon murmuring into the tiny plastic voice carrier, running again through the shocking details.

"There's some codeine in the bathroom cabinet," she told someone with a considerably less severe headache than my own. The throbbing in my temples reverberated against the windows.

The surgeon suddenly stepped through the door looking like a man playing the part of himself in a Hollywood movie: lantern-jawed, hairy-armed; he was dressed in short-sleeved greens. His oblong eyes were repellent with coagulated admonition, his wide nostrils jarred with the primary odours of life-or-death struggles.

When he looked down on us, I felt a mass gathering at the front of my brain.

"Are you Melanie's parents?"

I sat there, staring at him. My wife nodded.

For some strange reason I just wanted to hit him, to meet the threat head-on; I wanted to take him out before he could do any harm to us. Tears were running down my face, pattering softly into the carpet.

"Your daughter remains critical. She's lost a lot of blood, but right now she's being taken to the ICU. We think she's going to be OK."

His voice suddenly sounded beautiful. Looking at his smiling mouth felt like backing away from the grave. His smile became the centre of my universe; all irregular planes, all wonky angles and topsy-turvy landscapes, all perspectives and elementary outlines lay in the slice of his mouth: his miraculous, wonderful, smiling mouth.

"You understand she is still very ill...sliced the windpipe...but in time..."

I feared I would suffocate; my arm crawled around my wife's shoulder for support. She held my finger as though it was a steel spike, grounding her to what we were hearing, giving her purchase upon the future. Through the skill of his fingertips, the surgeon had severed the vaporous head of the Gorgon: he had brought our daughter back. I found myself squatting on my haunches, my eyes flushing like a toilet. My wife's soft scream disgorged into the room like a frightened wild animal suddenly relieved of its terror.

I didn't know what to do with myself. If I'd stood, I could have looked out of the hospital window at the city, I could have gazed into its filthy murderous maw. But as I rose to my feet, my wife took my hand firmly, as if I was a child wanting to cross a dangerous road. She leaned into me, pushing her head into my neck. I managed to clear my constricted throat. "Thank you doctor."

The surgeon nodded lightly and turned to leave.

"They'll let you see her soon," he said over his shoulder.

"Mr O'Leary," my wife said, taking a step towards him. "Thank you."

Her gaze fell upon him with sacramental tenderness, the air of her devotional breath brushed his face. He smiled and nodded, then turned back and strolled insouciantly down the corridor, slapping his thigh with his theatre mask. Behind him, his communicants lay prostrate, accepting his incarnational supremacy, his resurrectional theosophy.

For the first time in eight hours I started to breath more easily. I unclenched my buttocks and in the silence of the waiting room a sudden fart escaped my bowels like a thunderclap.

"Sorry. Irritable bowel's kicked off," I announced, sheepishly.

My wife looked at me, rubbing her nose and snuffling.

"Better out than in," she said.

I drew her to me and gazed into her pale-blue eyes. Then I kissed her.

"Let's snuggle up in one of the arm chairs. They'll come and fetch us soon."

As she nestled in my lap the rising sun sneaked over the window and silvered the grey wall of the waiting room. Within minutes, my adorable wife, the mother of our child, was curled up like a ball, asleep in my arms. I stroked her lustrous hair and listened for the inaudible sighs that gathered deep within her.

Outside, in the waking city, people were just leaving their beds. Radios and TVs were starting to blare, milk and fruit juices were being poured, bacon and eggs were being fried. A weary natural cycle over which we have no control was keeping its quotidian hours. The horrible, endless night was scurrying away to its cage and dawn was sitting up in bed.

As the hospital began to hum with its indecipherable encryption, I lowered myself further into the chair's outstretched arms, cuddled my wife and through a super-human effort of judo-throw will-power, forced the squinting rays of a new day into healing torn flesh.

# Goodnight Golgotha

Jonesy reached for the pill-jar and dropped his morning tab. Without the pills he became unstable; although he never used that exact word himself – unstable. Unstable sounded like 'mad'; it sounded...*Bad*. Jonesy preferred the word – *Borderline*. That word had a flavour of the Outlaw; of riding for your life through the dark and stormy night.

He dropped three spoonfuls of instant and four sugars into a mug, then inserted two slices of white into the toaster. Jonesy's toaster was feral and brutish; it was not a normal toaster. In a normal toaster, the bread is ejected on a spring mechanism when toasted. Jonesy's toaster no longer worked that way. Jonesy's toaster was trying to kill him.

When done, the bread would huddle down in the machine like cheese in a trap. Jonesy knew, if he wanted toast, he would have to fight for it. The fork was usually his best option. He had tried to fish the bread out with a knife once, but had touched some electrical element that had sent him flying across the kitchen on a sanguinary trajectory into the wine-rack. The mixture of cheap red wine and blood dripping on to the floor had magnified a whisper of childhood: a whisper of the power of conspirators.

The accident had set him on a journey back through the terrible museum of his past. Back to the Catholic rituals of his childhood, to the children's home and the mutilating memory of the priest taking him back to his house. The scene had unfolded like a well-planned homo-erotic novel: the smell of hot saliva, the explosion of fierce kisses and his terrified falsetto voice begging to be allowed to go. For a while he was obsessed by the idea of Christ returning to judge the wolves who preyed on children. Jonesy's bible-reading told him that Jesus had loved children, but he'd never quite believed it.

Then he began to turn religion in on itself. He began to believe that religion wasn't about love, that religion wasn't interested in right or wrong. He believed too, that religion protected its own – *'qui tacet consentit'*.

He was standing at his kitchen window, trying to focus on the horizon. From the eleventh floor council flat, the horizon was a long way off. His ill-fitting corporation window uncaringly admitted the undiluted heft of the city, as potent as gamma-rays. The city's rude slapstick, its absurd Comedie Humaine, intimidated him. The ever-expanding city wasn't his element, he didn't fit. He didn't know *how* to fit.

On a clear day, he could see all the way to the thin strip of brown water and the blocks of yuppy-*favelas* that marked the new development in the Bay. The exhilarating sophistication of the Bay, the normality of philanthropy, concordance, interchange, was only a bus-ride away, but Jonesy never went there; normality, cordiality, goodwill, were on the far edge of the world. The estate was Jonesy's world: the raging gulags with their fearful vortex of energies, their own un-laws, their inimical OTHERNESS.

This morning, the city quivered and warped into the distance where it was erased by the permanently dripping clouds that flew horizontally, like flapping grey spinnakers, straight at him. Jonesy's window was a kind of lens through which he interacted with the city. But even when he moved away from the window, he still carried the city with him as a kind of momentum, a perpetual motion that demoralised and exhausted him, affecting his mood; the city could leave him moping for days. He thought that the city should carry a warning label, like some mind-altering drug: THE CITY MAY INDUCE MELANCHOLY. CONSULT A QUALIFIED PSYCHIATRIST.

Sipping his coffee, Jonesy gazed down at the nervous, enmity-spitting streets. He thought he was lucky to be living on the edge of the estate, on the borders of the nether-world; a Pandemonium that churned out epic amounts of poverty and disadvantage. It was what they call a 'sink' estate. No, it was a lot worse than that; it was a Manhattan-style war-zone, with its body counts and cars burned out like battlefield hulks, the rising plumes of violence drifting overhead. A bundle of buildings TERRORISED and emptied of life, whose contentment had been vaporised into space. And there was always a lot more TERROR where that came from.

The used combustion rose in dense farts above the stalled traffic. As a spectator of traffic, Jonesy realised that some people, seized by a profound frustration from the lack of space, had reacted to the congestion by buying themselves huge military-style jeeps, some with tubular constructions welded to the front end to ward off anyone daring to make them slow down or brake for any reason. These demanders of *Lebensraum*, these AUTO-NAZIS squatted grimly in the fighting-compartments of their Range Rovers, Land Cruisers and Cherokees. Both men and women, especially the seventeen-year-old girls flicking cigarettes from the windows of their GTi's, found it unacceptable to sit for a moment of forced self-reflection. No interruption to the flow of energy could be tolerated.

Pouring himself another cup of the black coagulum he called 'coffee', Jonesy sat at his table and scanned the morning paper for something worth reading, even harbouring a strange idea that there would be something in it to cheer him. He should have known better. The paper was full of emotional thuggery, bursting with the malignity of human weakness.

He scanned a headline that slewed his thoughts and churned his stomach. It was pornographic; he was sickened with disgust: DRIVER KILLS EIGHT YEAR OLD GIRL.

"Oh, no. Oh, Christ no." Jonesy got up and returned to his position by the window. He looked out at the lines of traffic. The people sitting in their business-class comfort filled him with hatred. Beautiful secretaries, handsome salesmen, mothers with shopping, teenagers on their way to the sea-side, were killing children. Descending into despair, he started weeping softly. Then he shouted down at the lines of traffic:

"You stupid bastards! You're killing the kids!"

A great tear hung for a moment, trembling from the end of his nose, then fell like a bright meteorite, hitting the windowsill with a seismic splat. Like catatonic zombies, the commuters were sitting with glazed eyes, slouched in their private moments, ready to smile, or kill.

"They're killing the poor bloody kids," he moaned, crossing his arms and hugging himself like people do in cold weather. Looking up at the clock on his kitchen wall, Jonesy realised that the killing time had started. Drivers, late for work, were already unleashing their lethal pogroms on unsuspecting children. He watched the hands of the white-faced clock creep towards the safe-time of nine. The clock was white-faced because it anticipated the lunacy of the coming day.

Jonesy felt he should say a prayer for the eight-year-old girl. But then he said to himself, "Prayers don't work any more. Not any more." At least not the kind of prayers he said; the desperate, ill-thought-out prayers that are heard in prisons and shanty-towns, in bullet-riddled foxholes. Not the helpless, heart-tearing prayers that are heard outside the children's ward or the colliery gate. Those prayers don't work any more. Not any more. They never did.

It was too soon to pop another pill, but Jonesy felt lacerated, throbbing and bleeding inside. He ignored the pill-jar and picked up the Teachers; he was going to kick its arse good. After too many timid decisions, kicking the Teachers' arse at breakfast felt like an act of defiance.

The Scotch soothed like warm milk. "I'm sorry," he blurted out as he wiped the tears from his face with the back of his hand. "I'm sorry they're doing this to you." He knew he didn't have the power to change anything. Jonesy didn't know how power worked. But he knew how sorrow worked, and he was SORRY. He trembled with sorrow, it squatted in his eyes and ran from his nostrils; sorrow swelled in his throat, choking him and contorting his face. Boy did sorrow HURT…Ow, ow, ow.

Jonesy understood that sorrow was the true enemy, not pain, not loneliness, not death. Sorrow was the true onslaught, the real trial of strength. He'd fought with sorrow and lost, as usual. Now he'd crossed the breaking-line; sorrow had sucked the light from his eyes. He began to tremble and sweat; a wild-eyed anxiety attack was already working itself up.

The more he reflected on his life in the atavistic City, the more he appreciated its justness. The city was simply a modern equivalent of the ancient battleground for survival of the fittest. Lumbering four-wheel-drive machines were only another equivalence; they were genetically enhanced war elephants used to threaten and intimidate. What had he been thinking of? What possible sway could he have had here, with his effete theories on kindness, benevolence and respect for others?

"What can you do with this fucking world? You're losing it. You're losing it, pal."

He began to shake with fear, a flagellating fear, a fear that tore at his self-control like a wild beast. Jonesy was afraid of everything, and now fear had kicked down the door and unbuckled its belt; fear had boiling lips and a brazen leer; fear was wearing a holy vestment. Inside his head a small boy began weeping.

"Oh Christ…you've lost it TJ. You've fucking lost it."

He was right. His days were always numbered, now he'd lost it. Perhaps he'd never had it. He'd moved to the city to get away from the past, but the past kept re-making itself in its own image. Now it was ground-zero, the black-hole epiphany. Jonesy had finally had enough of his own internal wrangling, his own interminable end-gaming. He could feel his worthless life yawing away.

The night-time city went on quivering and sucking in energy and doing its city thing. Over in the Bay, in the garrulous restaurants, the diners savoured their overpriced wines. In the reverberating discos, prancing and flailing to ear-blistering music, the clean-jeaned gigolos flattered their inamoratas. In flat 1133 in the west-wing of Nye Bevan House on George Thomas Way, the music had stopped; the only sound was the low syncopation of the rain spotting the window with black stigmata. The biology of decay was already busy with him. Green-overalled medics, immune to disaster, had turned out to pick up the pieces, had yomped up the twenty-two flights of stairs, dragging themselves through swathes of old urine and bringing with them their attendant crowd of flickering-blue gawkers.

In his last hours Jonesy had faced death reluctantly: like the ancient zealot declared by others 'King of the Jews'; though, unlike the demi-god, he had departed life without the opiate of belief. Mercifully, there was no secular cross, no dreaded ascription hanging above his head. Out on the landing, the city began invoking its own kind of epitaph: more iconoclastic, less redeeming than the sacrificial INRI…

'You live next door. What was he like?'
'Don't know, never spoke to him.'

# Phrenics, Gluggers
and Fabulists

The homeless usually know in their hearts that they had a hand in their un-homing. Zak understood this (Richard was his given name but he had adopted the more heroic streetname of Zak) and used to reflect upon his disconnected past as he lay cocooned in his sleeping bag in some monoxide-filled vestibule.

Of course, there are multifarious reasons for anyone taking to living on the streets: drugs/booze addictions, marriage/relationship failures, social/mental inadequacies, etc. but, whatever the reasons, the un-homed are those who decide to flee the prevailing and drive out to some lonely spot to torch their pasts; ready to duel with what may come rather than be flattened by the present.

And then there's that popular misconception regarding homeless people: that they are in their predicament because they have abrogated their responsibilities. Nothing could be further from the truth; Zak prided himself on shouldering his share of any going burden. What attracted him to street-life had been its atemporal free-form dynamic, its obliqueness and utter disregard for chronology. The street offered him an escape from the atrophy and austerity of his mental malaise; the street's non-negotiable intolerableness and failed connections reflected his own steel-shuttered solitariness. Surviving on the street seemed, to Zak, to be an act of self-parody.

The truth was: Zak didn't really mind being homeless. The worst of it, for him, was the struggle to free himself from a warm bag and stand among the broken glass and smeared dog-shit to take a cold, post-apocalyptic late-night piss. Admittedly, being homeless included a certain lack of status for him, but he compensated for this by thinking of himself (with a great deal of chutzpah) as…an ENABLER.

Braving all weathers and for very inadequate money, he allowed, no…he HELPED people who were unfairly deprived of certain opportunities. He realised that there were many people out there who rarely got to experience the nobility of GIVING, or of offering a KINDNESS and even fewer people got to feel the blessedness of being spontaneously CHARITABLE. Yes, Zak had spotted a hole in the market: he could make people feel good about themselves at a negligible, even derisory, cost to themselves.

In his heart, Zak felt slightly inauthentic as a street-person; he'd never really taken to any kind of intoxication, – save for snatching the odd moment of incipient catatonia with a nugget of hash. He had his *sui generis* reasons for hitting the street, but didn't like talking about them. All he would say was that it was something to do with an endocrine imbalance. His condition was easily treated pharmacologically, but when left to itself, its symptoms could be highly disruptive, schizophreniform, even.

Zak spent the grotesque street-nights trying to find somewhere to bed down; usually some shadowy corner in the City's angry *Terra Incognita*. Or, sometimes he'd just walk the tiger-eyed-neoned streets, chatting to the outreach teams and the egregious social workers hunting down their mentally ungrounded 'clients' – a term he frankly despised – ready and eager to palliate the delusional and the depressive, the suicide time-bombs whose serotonin levels had dropped through the floor. These inaccessible 'clients' were the true unfortunates, their lives reduced to befuddled arse-wiping basics.

Dave was Zak's only friend. They liked each other on the sound basis of street expediency: they watched out for each other. Dave had no history of mental illness. He used to teach

French at a well-regarded comprehensive up in the Valleys. His command of the language was very good, though, nowadays, rarely used. Dave's wife had had an affair and then cheated him out of the house and then he'd started drinking and then he lost his job and then, finally…the *Diaspora*. The ex-teacher still had a towering thirst, though he never considered himself an alcoholic; in a nation of heavy drinkers, Dave thought he was just setting a higher standard of boozing. But despite all the glugging, the pot-bellied ball of a Welshman with the coruscating complexion of a fire-extinguisher proved to be a good friend to Zak. In fact, he'd tried desperately to save his life.

The two nomads had their favoured spot for their daily enterprises of sipping Bow and begging. It was at the top of Churchill Way where the wide road melds with the self-indulgent pavements of Queen Street. Just a few yards down from the corner, where the bank's cash machines spewed money into the hands of bad-tempered shoppers, they would sit on their mats, day-dreaming that some colluding hot-shot with too much money would drop two crisp Charles Darwins (tenners) into their outstretched hands. Of course, it never happened.

When not engaging Dave in misshapen dialogue of Beckettian absurdity, Zak used to like to stare into the faces of the passers-by. Some of the passing herd would completely blank him, afraid that by noticing him, they were in effect registering a relationship, however tenuous. Perhaps these people were afraid of contagion, he thought, afraid of catching failure or even Gurney-faced madness.

Others would communicate their devastating disapproval with a smile. These were the truly conceited and Zak despised their smiles. He daydreamed of strangling the smug bastards with their own silk ties and Hermes scarves.

And then there were those who appeared to Zak's jaundiced eye to be headed for their own street venues, their own piece of carpet and upturned hat. These were the stooped human gargoyles who were hung with their own harrowed distress. He could see the fear and mania in their furrowed faces; he could smell the demons from the pit that dragged them down, tearing at their flesh, turning their reasoning lobes into jelly.

It was for these people, the unviable, the auto-destructive, the terminally downward, that he reserved his worst contempt. These were the people who scared him; looking into their faces was too close to looking in a mirror.

Early one summer morning, Zak and Dave took up their usual positions and began talent-spotting the schoolgirls as they paraded by. Apart from the page-sticking Reader's Wives section he carried in his dilapidated rucksack,

71

this prurient activity and its consequential wanking session constituted the entirety of Zak's moribund sex-life.

Suddenly, and unbelievably to Zak, he heard one girl among a crowd of her friends say shrilly into a mobile phone: "I'm not surprised."

Zak's blood instantly boiled at this outrage.

"WHAT!" he shouted, loud enough for the girl to hear as she got level with him. "You're not surprised? At your age, EVERY-FUCKING-THING should surprise!"

The crowd of girls ran quickly past him, the one still trilling into her mobile phone. Dave hadn't heard what the girl had said, so he had no idea why Zak had just spontaneously exploded. He looked worriedly at his friend and barked, "Jesus, Zak. The way that girl jumped, I thought you'd pulled your cock out or something. And that is definitely the worst fucking chat-up line I've ever heard!"

Worse was to follow. Less than half an hour later Dave noticed a couple of guys mooching up the road from the direction of Cardiff gaol, one tall and long haired, the other a short shave-headed bull-like figure with his hands pushed down into his pockets, his head skulking down as he walked. This one looked pale, too pale. He had a plastic carrier bag scrunched under his arm; Dave guessed that he'd just been let out.

As they passed by, the tall one nodded at Zak.

"Alright lads?" Zak responded.

"Get a fucking job, you fucking PARASITES," the short guy snarled.

Dave just shook his head sorrowfully, he'd taken that kind of shit a hundred times before, and so had Zak. But not today, not on this beautiful summer's morning. No way, Zak wasn't taking that kind of shit today.

"Fuck you, arsehole!" Zak shouted at the guy's back.

The short guy stopped, turned and glared at him for a second.

"For fuck's sake leave it, Skaggsy," said the taller guy, tugging at his friend's arm. "Oh Christ, not AGAIN!"

It was too late. The shave-headed pit-bull dropped his plastic bag and jumped at Zak, teeth bared, snarling and spitting. Zak hardly had time to get to his feet before the guy's forehead smashed into his nose. He heard a faint click as the cartilage splintered and then he dropped like a sack of cement.

When Zak's head hit the pavement, it sounded to Dave like a water melon had been dropped from rooftop height. The two guys were already more than a hundred yards away by the time Dave lifted his friend's head from the concrete. Both his hands pooled with warm blood and blobs of cerebrum.

"Oh no…not you, Zak. Please, not you."

People continued to walk past, hurrying from the scene of TOO MUCH REALITY that shocked and frightened them. They scurried away, wrapping themselves in their *nearly* lives, their partial and insecure fuck-'em-all lives.

"Call an ambulance!" Dave screamed. "Call a fucking ambulance!" Then he saw that Zak's face was changing colour; he was turning blue.

"Oh shit! Don't die, Zak. Don't die!"

He shook off his coat and placed it under his friend's shattered head. Then he reverted to type. His training in schoolyard resuscitation kicked in. He pulled Zak's tongue from the back of his throat and began blowing air into his friend's deflated lungs.

It was only moments later that the ambulance arrived and within minutes they were pulling into the jazzy A+E department that had been bolted on to the side of the Gothicy Infirmary. Zak was quickly stripped from his clothes and examined by the triage team. They took him straight to the I.C.U. and connected him to a machine that took care of his breathing for him.

All Dave could do was wait. He remained surprisingly calm and after finding a toilet to wash away the blood and divots of his friend's brain, a nurse came and settled him into the relatives' waiting room. Later, she gave him a cup of sweet tea. She was an attractive 'full figured' girl and her name-badge spelled: GENEVIEVE.

"Nice name," Dave said.

"Thanks." She smiled. "Try not to worry to much, your friend is in good hands. I'm sure he'll pull through."

What a smile, Dave thought, and wondered what lucky bastard she'd be going home to that night; whose firm shoulder would she lean on after tottering in after a stress-filled day at work?

"There's no fucking justice in this world," he muttered.

And then he became aware of his own smell. It was a putrid appley kind of smell, tinged with other denser stinks: he needed some soap badly. He wished there was a shower in the waiting room – or, better still, a decon-tamination unit. Dave glanced down at the cast of his blood-smeared coat. Besides the organic residue, the material was covered with small black fag-burn holes, giving it the appearance of a well-used rifle target. The right sleeve had a long tear down it that was clinched together with shiny brown packing tape.

He realised that he was a reeking shell of the man he'd once been. With shaking hands and piquant horror, Dave saw himself as he truly was: a weak, disgraceful, over-qualified drunk. He felt as if he were here, in this hospital waiting room, to witness his own blood-soaked coup-de-grace.

"I know," he muttered to himself. "Enough is enough."

Stolidly, he snuggled himself down into the plastic coated armchair and listened to the hubbub of ringing telephones, clattering trolleys and slopping mops. He tried to relax; he knew he wasn't going anywhere soon.

Of course, they did all they could for Zak. But it was a hopeless endeavour. The brain surgeons agreed that even if he survived the operation, he'd be an onion-head: a poor excuse for a vegetable. So they let him go. Although his kidneys lived on.

During his cider-fuelled maunderings, Dave hoped that the transplant recipient sometimes thought about his friend, the donor. Then, bursting a few more facial capillaries, he'd turn his ruddy face skywards and brandish his fist at the heavens.

"And how are you feeling you dispassionate MOTHER-FUCKER? Pretty good I suppose." Dave attached a particular importance to calling HIM names. He used to be a lay preacher, so he knew all about HIS wrath…

"Au plaisir de vous revoir, you COCK-SUCKER!"

Two years later, when Dave had tired of sleeping in cardboard boxes and getting biffed about by hooligans, he finally left the streets and got himself cleaned up. It took him a while to get used to sleeping in a room that didn't resemble a bus-station, but he adjusted to it and got used to sleeping on clean white cotton stretched almost to transparency over a comfortable mattress. He even managed to overcome his lackadaisical attitude to food, sitting down to meat, green vegetables and potatoes like some prosaic middle-class paterfamilias.

A daily mega-dose of Seroxat acted as a breakwater against the great inundations of despair that still engulfed him; the drug also helped him to get his drinking under some sort of control. He tried to temper his glugging so that a good night's sleep was the only oblivion the booze provided.

Even so, he would sit for hours at his table, glaring at a bottle of cheap sherry while fingering the plastic foil that held his pills. Was the tightness he felt in his stomach a side-effect of the anti-depressants, or was it the anxious anticipation that he was beyond the help of the sunlight chemicals he held in the block of his hand? When he looked at his friend-cum-enemy across the table, he tried to imagine its seductive curves as a murderous face, with curled red lips and distended fangs. Then he'd have to shake his head to dispel the terrifying vision.

Truthfully, he could no longer remember why his frantic coupling with the booze had begun. What spinning darkness had descended to kick-start the engine of his terrible thirst? The landscape of his past as a teacher was so distant now that it seemed to have the appearance of someone else's nostalgia. The past was a handful of dust, its truth was…nothing, its reality was…nothing.

Dave had been a very happy drunk. He'd used laughter as a way of coping with conflict, using it as a substitute for aggression. Even when he had walked in on his wife in bed with another man, he'd said, "Hang on, there's something funny going on here." Laughter was Dave's defence: it seemed that the saying 'I didn't know whether to laugh or cry' was tailor-made for Dave.

Anyway, Dave knew that depression was rage turned inwards and that now he felt his anger had been attenuated, he could commence his life proper. At the moment he realized this, a surge of adrenaline rushed through his body, washing his muscles and loaded nerves: the dizziness of being-in-the-world threatened to overwhelm him. Dave began to dance around his flat, laughing like a schoolboy at playtime. He even forgot about his daily visit to the off-licence.

One Sunday morning, in a moment of perception, Dave discovered that he needed some predictability in his life, so he reconnected with the church that he had so vehemently driven away. No matter how hard he'd tried to avoid it, he was closely involved with the bucking-bronco life that God had given him; it was his life, it was personal, so he'd better get on with it.

He was glad to be back in the Church; he was in a nearly constant state of euphoria – he developed the habit of juxtaposing the loathsomeness of street-life with the delectable sensation of fellowship and eagerness-of-greeting he found amongst his fellow Christians. To them, Dave was an appealing character (despite his waiting for the moment of silent prayer before sending a deafening fart heavenwards). He'd actually had real and violent experience of godlessness, witnessing death at its ugliest. But he had finally come back to the Church. Dave told everyone it was because he was hoping for a new start; and everyone liked him for it.

And not only did Dave embrace the Church, he embraced one of its male parishioners. Dave fell in love with another man. To begin with, he was profoundly uneasy with the situation – he thought that maybe his hysterical glugging had re-arranged his emotional molecules; maybe the street's craziness had reversed his sexual polarities. Or maybe he'd always been queer. But when he calmly considered all the forlorn by-ways and soul-depressing cul-de-sacs that had brought him to this position, he figured that any love was good love and he had had enough experience of no-love to know about these things. So he was pleased to limit the suicidal boozing and confine himself to

79

those less taxing elixirs of life...love and affection.

It then occurred to Dave that he had been in love with his good friend Zak; although he had never, even in the depths of his imagination, had a single homosexual thought about him. It was as if some delicacy or balance had to be maintained. It was a juggling act that Dave didn't understand.

Dave's new partner has some of the fussiness and aloof neatness of the high camp – the carefully drawn up weekly menu is the focus of many an emotional confrontation – but he reckons it's a perfect counterbalance to his own ramshackle habits and wilful neglect. Sometimes the two saunter up to the cemetery off the A48 at Culverhouse Cross and lay yellow and white flowers on Zak's grave. It helps Dave to remember – and then, for months, not to remember at all.

# The Love Disease

Sometimes it's fatal.

Sometimes it even kills.

Love, I mean. I mean, the love disease.

If it's true what they say, that love is always a fiction, then that last chapter of my life was written by Stephen Blood-Bath King.

*Bring it on, Stevie boy, give it to me in the chest with both barrels...*

*YOU CRAZY, DEMENTED SICKO – you'll get no plea-bargaining here.*

It was my own fault. Well, I panicked didn't I? bloody panicked. Usually, we (us males) just experiment with love. We sort of try it on for size, check it out, take it for a test drive; or just sit back for a while and see how comfortable the thing feels. Then, of course, we decide that it was the other thing, or model or shape or colour, that we wanted all the time.

But this was something new; this time around, I fell for a Squeeze like tripping head first down the stairs. I'd been on my own for too long, I suppose. You can always tell when you've been on your own for too long because your gaff starts taking on a look like the inside of Fagin's pocket, and worse, things start getting a bit KINKY; things start getting a bit TWISTED. Like your neighbour's washing line suddenly becomes interesting.

You start gazing dreamily at the frilly white bits, you know what I mean. Then your hand sieves down into your jeans and the old snake's-head gets some cramped physiotherapy. I mean, Jesus – a fucking hand-job over an EMPTY pair of bloody knickers – I ask you!

I was so desperate for a shag, I even considered buying one of those blow-up sex-dolls. But when I read the blurb on the box, I had immediate doubts: 'LIFE-LIKE! REALISTIC!' I knew, as soon as I blew some life into her, the plastic bitch would start nagging me about being a no-hope fucking loser, and then make me sleep in the spare bed. So fuck the sex-dolls.

Anyway, it turned out that Renee and I had something in common. It was an alcohol thing. Oh, we didn't know it then but we both had a big problem with the alcohol. It's like…like some lingering illness that never goes away, and then it gets you. The concentration loss, the trembling, the sweats: the booze always gets you in the end. And that's when the FUN starts…

I have no idea why, but at some youthful evolutionary stage, the two excitements, the twin jollies – booze and women – became inextricably linked in my subconscious. Meeting Renee was like a destiny fulfilled, a dream come true. She seemed perfect for me. I had found that mythical woman, that holy grail: a big handsome babe who loved to FUCK and BOOZE.

Now I'm just another long-haired, round-shouldered loser with an alcohol thing. Yeah, you got it – I'm a Literary Lion, a fucking writer. And as though it's not enough to be entwined with booze and words I had to meet up with her. The problem was we were fast taking up residence in Dipsomaniaville, but thank God I didn't hang around that long. I had to let her go.

To tell you the truth it just got too mad, too weird. There was just too much Static and Violence. It all got too fucking NIHILISTIC.

What is it with the alcohol thing anyway? Why can some people take it or leave it and some of us can't stop ourselves taking it – and then some. It must be a gene thing. I guess we just happen to have genes that love to get pissed. I've always wondered why the human mind jumps at every opportunity to flee itself, pissed, stoned, high. What is it about the psyche that can't stand itself, can't even bear being in the same bony room as itself?

When I first saw her, she must have had the drinking under control. Even so, she still looked like a Metallica groupie that had run out of shelf-life. Except for her eyes. I could tell that her eyes liked to laugh; they would gleam like high-watt bulbs on a power surge. Her eyes were as blue as the sky: the poor asthmatic, ozone depleted totally fucked-up sky.

The thing was, she was just amazing to look at. When she sauntered over and sat next to me in the pub, she smiled politely and arranged herself with that female folding of limbs that all men find completely irresistible. I became fascinated by her. Despite her frightening Gothic fundamentalism, she was overwhelmingly feminine. To me, she looked perfect. Unfortunately, like all perfect things, she was destined for destruction. (As are all imperfect things!) The first thing she ever said to me was, "I'm bored." But I decided that what she meant was, "I'm lonely."

...And so began my tragic and painful descent to love.

Before I met Renee, drinking was a hobby, like football. Every weekend I'd kick the shit out of the booze and that was that for another week. But drinking became something else after meeting Renee. Getting pissed became full-time: passionate, uncontrollable. Everything we did together was interesting, even if we did it a hundred times. It was the booze you see, the booze made everything seem interesting. And because it made us feel young again, it didn't matter. You crashed out for days on end, then you just got up and did it all again. Time didn't matter.

That old booze slips its hand in your pocket then winds itself around your life. It eats your day and chews it into helpless hours. Take a tip from me, Bro, when you get mugged by the drink, it takes much more than just your money: it takes your WHOLE fucking LIFE too. And when you live like that, pretty soon you've got a situation; pretty soon you're going to find yourself up Shit Creek.

It happened to us in Tesco. Bloody Tesco – I ask you!

Un-fucking-believable!

Well, she'd sort of got a bit unstable by then, she was, how shall I put it? As mad as a shithouse rat.

So there we were, lushed up in Tesco and with our heads full of THC and feeling a bit randy, so we did it. Oh come on…gimme a break, you must've done it in some WEIRD places too. We were both smashed and horny so she dragged me into the Ladies for a quickie. Renee thought that humping in a Tesco toilet would make an amusing addition to our distinguished repertoire of sexual praxis. (We were already big with cinema seats and park benches.)

A sex-session with Renee is like three hours of high-impact aerobics; you're left rumpled, knackered, smelly and befuddled. Making love with her makes you feel like you are growing old at a hundred times the normal rate.

My orgasms with her were different, uncanny. Sex transcended itself from the usual male etiquette, the great iron-clad male tradition of 'me first'. When we made love, instead of the customary full-on selfishness, the hyper-sensitivity of the guy's personal 'come', I would find myself, how can I say?... sort of slowly rising on a bubble of intense awareness, savouring every moist touch and thrilling breath.

I would marvel at how incredibly lucky I was to be making love to this wonderful girl, this sexual encyclopaedia stuffed full of Woman's GENIUS for giving pleasure. Her lovemaking was a gift of sublime and guileless generosity.

Renee had the learned gifts of a carnal polymath; she was coital cognoscenti, a genius of the climax, a sexual prodigy. By her own admission, SHE NEVER SAID NO. Her favourite line as we fell into bed was:

"What's on the top of your sex-menu tonight then, lover boy?"

That line always had the effect of passing an electric current along the entire length of my explosively infatuated cock. And I recall she'd once asked me, in all seriousness, "Have you ever fainted when you come?"

"No. I don't think so," I stammered. "Would I remember?"

She kissed me hard, like a hot tyre sucking at a wet road, and said, "Keep the smelling salts handy, lover."

Only once before had sex ever got close to being that skilful, that enthusiastic, and by God that particular girl was worth EVERY penny I paid her; that girl would do anything for a hefty tip. But getting my leg over with Renee was something else, it was different, non-profit-making, more romantic – it was making love.

Renee gave me something that every man yearns for in bed: CONFIDENCE. The sort of wonderful, unpierceable confidence that blows away the cold mist of performance paranoia, the cock-shrinking self-consciousness that runs to nervous and erectile breakdown. When I hopped in the sack with her, I seemed to pull on a handsomely tanned and virile mask, then I'd cartwheel off into a delirium of impossibly lewd sexual gymnastics, and who the Hell needs Viagra's twenty-four hour triumphal hard-on when you're…*Making Love?*

What did I do for her? Well, I taught her multiplication. As we made love, I used to recite the nine-times table to try and delay the rapid onset of 'the point of no-return', that graceless anti-discharge scuffle with my knob that always seemed particularly hair-triggered with Renee. She used to sing rhythmically along with me…. "Nah nah nah, Nah nah nah." Then, "Hey! You're lasting longer. But do three times nine really make twenty-seven?" Thank God for my orgasm though: without that comma, without that pause, bugger all else would have got done.

I think I remember Renee saying that sex with me was "…invigorating, refreshing, like taking a very quick shower." That can't be true, can it? Probably.

Anyway, there we were, drilling away in the Tesco's Ladies, and then she started in on a blowjob. So I was sat on the throne and she was down there with her head going up and down like a pneumatic road-drill, her tongue heading for a terminal case of repetitive strain injury, when there was this tapping on the door. I completely lost the plot. I began to giggle. But she just continued to toil away, her head going up and down with lots of slurping and gurgling, like she was giving high-powered fellatio to a stick of Barry rock. The tapping got louder and louder, and my chuckles began to feed on themselves until they became a sphincter-bursting laugh.

She suddenly stopped and looked up at me quizzically. Completely ignoring the now irate banging on the door she asked: "What's the matter? What the fuck are you laughing at?"

I screamed with laughter. She loosened her grip on my unstable rod and threw it against my heaving belly. "What the fuck's wrong with you?" she spat. It took a phenomenal effort for me to calm down enough to answer. I really couldn't believe that anyone in their right mind could do what she was doing while someone was banging on the toilet door trying to get in.

"I can't believe you can still do that," I whimpered.

"What? What?" She was now getting very angry.

I managed to splutter, "I can't believe you're doing THAT, when some TWAT is banging on the door trying to get in! What the fuck are you, some kind of smack-head HOOKER?"

Thank God the security guard broke the door down when he did. The red in her face had deepened to that of the Earth's core. I could feel the temperature of her blazing anger – I had totally Fucked the Fuck-fest; BLOWN the BLOWJOB.

Well, a good laugh is as good as a blowjob, innit. Innit? Suppose it depends, eh? Anyway, by this time let's forget rigid, by now we're talking major flaccid; I mean as slack as a spaniel's ear.

The security guy had started pulling on my legs as I held on to the flush handle like grim death. "You're coming with me you dirty little bugger!" he was shouting.

"I'm not coming at all now, you stupid bastard!" I cried. (By the way, if ever you think your prong is small – just give it a bloody good scare. THAT is small.)

The heat from Renee's anger was super-stellar. She had started to BEAT THE SHIT out of me. Uh! Oh! – Game On! This was Life or Death stuff.

She was biting and scratching like a wounded lion on speed. My drunken Squeeze was snapping at my tackle like a dwarf alligator. It felt like she'd lunged at my cock with a broken bottle.

"Please don't *hurt* my knob!" I was screaming. "That's all I ask."

My gonads feared for their safety and clawed their way up into my belly. Renee had pushed the big red button; she'd gone fucking NUCLEAR.

When the security guard finally dragged me out of there I was covered in bites and cuts, and my prong felt and looked like a chewed toffee. I was covered in SNOT and BLOOD. It was grisly.

The security guys bundled me out of the store, arm and head-locked like I was some terrorist MOTHER-FUCKER.

"Hey, hey. Where are your fucking manners?" I croaked in a strange reedy voice. "What's happened to everyone's sense of humour?"

I also mumbled some half-choked things about 'grubby facilities' and 'dissatisfied customer' and 'seeking recompense'. That kind of thing. I think I made my point without losing too much dignity. They were using some kind of legal language, talking about 'DEVIANT behaviour' and 'dropping the net on this PERVERT'.

Now I don't know all the pros and cons about being a DEVIANT, but I do know this: the last thing a DEVIANT wants is to be brought into the SYSTEM.

Bang! There goes your fucking LIFE.

So there I was – INJURED and on the run.

I did love her, though. Honest I did, even through all that surreal crap. Well, love is stubborn, innit? I remember thinking a few nights later – she must be feeling it badly too. Missing me, I mean. I could imagine her lying on a floor somewhere, her anguished sobs flecking the night like snarling tracer-bullets.

Poor tormented kid. It's a tricky thing…Love.

# The Corrupted

Another August Bank Holiday weekend; early morning, with a light sea-mist creeping up the deserted streets from the glassy waters of the Bristol Channel. Thousands of car-engines are about to be revved up. The fiery anuses of aggrandising Beemers and scrap-iron MOT failures will belch ozone-disrespecting farts on to the damp tarmac. The summer morning's freshness is to be wounded with cavalier disdain. For the next few hours, Cardiff will be enjoying the same air quality as Mexico City.

Everyone is getting ready for the annual petrol-swilling stampede to the sea. They're headed for the beaches of the Gower or further west to Pembrokeshire's decontaminating, fresh-air benevolence.

By noon, the wild-eyed, hysterical mass of refugees jam the city's streets until they hit the M4 link-road. Then, taking off at ninety miles an hour, they drive as though they're on the inside straight at Brand's Hatch, barreling along until they get stuck in the first monster hold-up five miles up the road.

Then the sandwiches and economy-sized Coke bottles are brought out. After half an hour of sitting in the stationary traffic, amid the boil-overs and minor accidents, travel-sick kids are puking on to their shorts-clad, beach-ready legs. In front passenger seats, thousands of wives and mothers are swearing that Bank Holidays 'are more bloody trouble than they're worth'.

All have one single idea – to snag themselves a patch of noisy, crowded sand on which to broil themselves for a few hours; and then repeat the same interminable drag home. The army of eco-gobblers sit for hours in their stationary cars, yelling at the tops of their voices, "Die, ozone layer. Die!"

And the reason I'm ranting on about all this motoring madness is because I'm a fifteen-year on-the-job traffic cop.

The last time I took the wife and kids out into that antipathetic Bank Holiday mêlée, some total dildo with a car-full of adolescent thugs followed us with his radiator grill kissing our back bumper. When we reached some traffic lights he screeched up beside us and the front passenger leaned out of his window and howled, "Hey scumbag, you drive like a twat!"

My wife put her hand to her mouth, hardly believing what she'd just heard, then screamed at him, "We've got kids in the car!"

"Fuck you," was the instantaneous reply. "And fuck the kids."

Right then, the lights changed and they shot off in a cloud of burning rubber, with V-signs waving out the windows and an empty beer can lobbed back in our direction.

I turned around and looked at my kids. They were sat there like a couple of owls caught in a searchlight, trembling and close to tears. Now I was a respectable guy and I denounced all forms of violence, but if you picked on my family, there were likely to be some serious casualties. I wished I'd had a pump action shotgun clipped to the dashboard.

"Ring your friends down at the station." Anne was screaming and shaking with anger; she was vibrating with rage.

"No need. I've got his number," was all I said.

Naturally, I'd made a mental note of the zoo-on-wheels registration; and I'd got a good look at the passenger's face. I promised myself, 'I'll catch up with them – soon.'

That ugly scene was to be a tuning point for us all, although, at the time, none of us knew it.

The following Sunday, when my brother Andrew and his wife came over for lunch, Anne told them about it. After we'd eaten, my brother nodded to me to take our beers out into the garden.

"Just going out the back to smoke a panatela, love," I said casually, then followed Andrew out.

"What are you doing about that shit?" he asked. "You must have got their number." There was venom in his voice.

"Yeah, I got it."

"So. What are you doing about it?"

"Leave it to me, Andrew, I'll catch up with them."

"Have you looked it up on the computer? Where does the fucker live?"

"Andy. I can handle it."

"You know you'll need some help sorting those wankers, don't you?"

"I can handle it," I insisted.

"Jesus, Rob. Get those blinkers off, I deal with scum-bags like those guys everyday. While you're out there picking up road-kill off the motorway and handing out speeding tickets, I'm the one mixing it on the street with those misbegotten drug-dealing bastards, remember?"

"OK, OK. Don't rub it in," I snapped.

Andrew was a detective sergeant with the city's Drug Squad. I had been trying for a transfer to the same unit for two years but wasn't getting anywhere. It was a sore point between us. He reckoned I was better off nicking motorway pranksters and drunk-drivers. "Trust me Rob," he'd said, "you don't want to be dropped into the stinking menagerie I have to immerse myself in every day. Chasing those shit-head dealers can get dangerous. Those fuckers will shred your face with a broken bottle just for giggles."

But now, I was standing in my garden, looking at a forest-fire of rage in my brother's eyes. Conceding, I said, "OK Andy, what do you think I should do?"

"Not here...not today. We'll talk next week, when you come over to us. I want you to meet a couple of friends of mine."

"What friends? What's all this about?"

"It's about getting those arse-holes off the street for a while. We'll teach them to start in on your wife and kids."

"Bloody hell, Andy. What are you into?"

"Just come with an open mind next Sunday. We'll have a barbie. OK?"

"Yeah...OK...next Sunday."

"Good. Let's go back inside."

The morning of the barbie came around happily dressed in its sunglasses and sunhat. When I got down for breakfast, the kids were flip-flopping around in their bathers and plastic sandals. Anne was wearing a white linen dress that I could see her panties through when she bent over or when the streaming sunlight caught her in its X-ray clarity.

97

Despite having had early-morning sex with her just an hour or so ago, when she leaned over the table to clear the dishes, the full curves of her hips and bum gave me an instantaneous hard-on. Our earlier session had been the mechanical, lock-the-door, don't-make-any-noise kind of sex that married people like to call 'making love.'

After thirteen years of married life our intimacy was now defined by such interactions: the writhing acknowledgement, the half-hearted reminders, that we still shared a bed. Like idiot twins we knew each other's bodies inside out, knew each other's furtive secretions; Anne's swollen vagina, stretched to tearing by multiple childbirth, my own indiscreet poot-pooting arse-hole, voiding and honking while we humped and sweated amongst the twisted sheets.

But now, I fantasised about hoiking her dress up over her head and bending her over the kitchen table, thrusting into her moist honey-pot like the piston of a steam engine, while her fists pound the pine planks of the trembling table. In my porno-imagination she was screaming at the top of her voice, "God-all-Mighty that's good. Harder. Fuck me harder."

Why is it that love inevitably wears out over time, becomes boring routine, a dull catalogue of thrills that have palled? Taking its place – the inane conversations, the pointless arguments wadded with nonsense, the mechanical clinches; a clitoris barely tilted, the grinding prong dutifully assuaged.

So instead of grabbing hold of her in the kitchen, I placed my empty coffee-mug down on the table and patted her on the bottom as I passed. She didn't laugh, smile, or even say anything. I decided to go upstairs for my shower, and to jerk-off the head of steam I'd built up. Going up to the bathroom, I told myself morosely: "That's what two affection-competing kids and the familiarity of thirteen years of marriage does for your sex-life."

A Sunday afternoon barbecue at Andrew's; the two wives stacking up a groaning patio-table with enough salad and bread rolls to feed a herd of browsing elephants, the four kids yelping and running around on the lawn like a pack of dogs let loose on the beach. Andy and me constantly turning burgers and sausages, getting quietly but seriously drunk on ice-cold beer and tumblers of rum and coke.

We were sitting out in my brother's garden, watching the kids fighting over the control-console of a battery-powered truck, when I heard some strange voices. Looking back at the house, I saw Andy's patio was filling up with three burly guys, each clutching a can of booze to his generous belly. I could tell at a glance: his Drug Squad friends.

After three bone-crushing handshakes, the guys spread themselves out on the grass, sitting around me and Andy like a circled wagon-train.

For the first five minutes, Andrew did all the talking, mostly shop stuff, moaning about the drug-squad superior officers, the avalanches of paperwork they were tied down with, and other standard cop-whinges. The guys eyed me warily as Andy prattled on.

"So, what's happening?" I asked no-one in particular.

Andy looked over at the biggest guy of the group. The guy stared at me intently before speaking.

"I'm going to tell you a little story, Rob, and it's a true story, every bloody word of it."

I nodded and sat back in my chair.

"Six months ago, one of our boys nicked a supplier, not a street dealer, one of the big players. A few weeks later a gang chased our boy while he was coming out of the pictures with his girlfriend. They caught him and beat the shit out of him. He almost died. And to top it off, they gave his girlfriend a slapping as well."

"One of the bastards bit a chunk out of our friend's leg the size of your fist." Andy was almost spitting blood himself. "The bastards are looking out for each other by targeting the squad."

"They're fucking cannibals..." said the big guy, "...and it's not just us that risks violence now. They're a threat to our families, our wives and kids."

Andy leaned forward and put his hand on my knee.

"Rob, we're fighting back. We're taking the bastards on."

Just then, as if on cue, Anne came over with a tray-full of paper plates, plastic cutlery and napkins.

"Come on, Rob, Andy, get cooking. Everyone's waiting for their lunch."

As Andy and I walked towards the barbecue, he hissed at me, "We're going to sort out those morons that gave it to you and Anne."

I couldn't believe what I'd just heard from the lips of my own brother, a fellow cop.

"Andy! For fuck's sake. We're supposed to know the difference between the good guys and the bad guys."

"The system is on its last legs, Rob, you know that. If the city's scumbags are starting to target us, then we're just trying to equal things up."

"Equal things up? Who the hell are you, Dirty-fucking-Harry?"

I realised that we were shouting at each other. The guys sitting on the grass were looking at us and frowning. The big guy put his finger to his lips.

"Look, after what we've told you today, you're in whether you like it or not. Now give me the moron's address." Andy put out his hand.

"I've only got the driver's details."

"No matter. We'll find the others after we've visited the driver."

"My note-book's in the car. I'll have to fetch it."

"Do it now," Andy insisted. He was probably afraid that if I had time to think, I'd change my mind. He was right, too.

The following night, I called Andy up and told him I didn't want anything to do with his hit-squad. I was backing out. He just laughed, and told me it was too late.

I didn't need to look for the dick-head driver's block of flats. As soon as I drove into the estate I spotted it straight away. The ground floor flat was hard to miss. All of the windows had been smashed and debris littered the grass in front of the tower-block – broken glass, bits of clothing, pieces of splintered furniture, a shattered TV, doors ripped from their hinges.

I stepped up to one of the windows and looked inside. Sprayed in big red letters across the lounge wall was 'Don't fuck with women and kids'. All the other walls had been defaced with 'Scum'.

As I turned away, an old guy stepped out of the gloomy hallway next to the flat. "The blokes that did it were wearing balaclavas," he mumbled. "They were like animals, smashing the place up."

I just pulled a sad face, and nodded.

"They took the lad away in an ambulance."

I raised my eyebrows, as though to say, 'Tell me more'.

"I heard the kid's in a bad way over at the Heath. Two broken legs."

Again I just nodded. Then raised a palm as I walked away. I hadn't said a word, but I'd got all the information I needed. I was in a state of complete shock.

I knew that the other morons would have had a hiding too. I called Andy on his mobile and told him I had to see him – NOW! We met in a pub car-park.

"I've just been to see what you arranged with your friends. What the hell's happened to you, Andy? What kind of law enforcement is beating the crap out of people?"

"It's the law of the tooth and the fang, Bro. Anyway, the fat is in the fire and it's too late to pull it out again."

For the next few minutes there was silence between us. I was seething. We both gazed out of the car's windows at the passing traffic. Then Andy looked at his watch and opened the car door.

"I'm sorry you feel that way, Rob. I had plans for you to join us on the squad. There's a vacancy coming up. Anyway, I'm off. I've wasted an hour already." He looked at me with a half grin and walked back to his own car.

"Call me when you've calmed down!" he shouted over his shoulder.

That same afternoon, I helped to cut a father and his dead child from a wrecked car on the M4 near Newport. It was gruesome. Those are the kind of heartbreakingly cruel scenes that give God a bad name. But then again, I suppose that bad driving, like earthquakes and tsunamis, are none of God's business.

It always tore me to pieces when there were kids involved in those fatals. The fraudulent promise of a life, the body that was theirs and not theirs, the lightning-quick rearranging of a newly-formed anatomy. Those poor kids, I didn't want to share their insides with them; their hideous rib-cages, their purple intestines; the voiding shit and piss. Something went wrong inside my head, some nervous thermostat, some gawky regulator of my repose was blown. My memory banks were full of reminders of my own children's corporeality, and I had no resistance left.

After every one of those call-outs, I'd go home and pet my kids, kiss them and tell them that I loved them. But nothing could assuage the dismal end-of–the-world feeling, the full-on awareness of their vulnerability. I was constantly being made aware that at some point our children abandon us, one way or another.

When I got home that night, I just sat at the kitchen table and drank the best part of a half-bottle of whisky. Anne didn't say anything, she guessed what had happened. I always hit the bottle after witnessing a fatality. I didn't tell her about them any more, but I did tell her about the hiding that had been arranged for the Morons. She was upset that their friends might try to hit back at us. Of course there was no way – they wouldn't even know who'd done it. But Anne had always been nervous about being left alone at nights, and she tried to persuade me to have a burglar alarm fitted.

"Bloody hell, love," I joked, trying to reassure her. "Those guys would have to be real bloody psychos to break into a working copper's house. Especially with a retired German Shepherd police-dog, a cat, a budgie, two kids that never sleep, a goldfish and a hamster called Shrek to let you know there's a stranger in the house. If you don't wake up with that lot going off, a burglar alarm would be what we crime professionals call a complete and utter waste of fucking time."

Later, I promised her that we'd get one fitted.

As I lay in bed that night, I couldn't stop thinking about the young girl's broken body lying in the twisted wreckage of that car. Traffic cops see some desperately bad things, some horrible sights. I didn't know how much longer I could go on making a living like that.

The job was starting to upset me, give me the creeps; maybe I was getting too old.

It was then the suspicion crept into my mind: I was going over the hill, losing my edge. The worst thing was I didn't feel tragic at all, just weary. Bone weary. Maybe that's why I decided to cross the line, whatever the line was.

The last thing I thought about before sleep reluctantly found me was the hiding that Andy and the drug-squad boys had given to the Morons. As I lay there, mulling it over, I whispered internally to myself, "Well, at least there was no buggering around with a load of paperwork. And those morons weren't worth a pot of piss anyway."

The next day, I was still in shock about what Andy had done, but not the kind of shock I had expected. A strange feeling coursed through me. A lightness of spirit perhaps; or even, if I'm perfectly honest, a little glee. A line from a movie kept leaping into my head: *I know what you're thinking punk...did he fire only six shots, or was it seven? Well...go ahead punk. Make my day.*

As I drove through town to work, I realised that I had taken some sort of plunge. I had decided to defend myself and my family from all-comers. If nothing else, it gave me a sense of empowerment, of being in the 'Don't fuck with me' league.

I called Andy to smooth things over. I told him I was OK with the situation, but he didn't want to discuss it over the phone so we arranged to meet for a few drinks down at the police club that night. When I got there, he was sat amongst a group of his drug-squad cronies. They sat together with the familiar assurance of men who have sat thus many times before.

The gang were a hearty, fart-powered production of mateyness. Taking in the picture of shiny, sweaty, laughing testosterone, I decided to get myself a pint and to sit down on the edge of the group. I wasn't getting into a round with that boozy lot; it would cost me a fortune.

The guys were getting drunk with the usual cacophony of male discourse, discussing male-pattern baldness, offering pitilessly crude stories about ex-girlfriends and telling jokes. One of the lads was telling a Blunkett story; when the laughter died down, Andy looked over at me and waved a hand, pointing to the bench seat beside him. As I squeezed in he leaned over and asked, "Everything OK?"

"Yeah. Everything's fine."

"You sure?"

I just nodded and took a sip from my pint.

"You're OK with it, yeah?"

I looked at my brother and gave him a huge grin.

"I'm very OK with it, Andy."

"Good. In that case I've got some news for you."

Andy held up his glass as if to make a toast.

"Gentlemen, I present to you my Bro. He's joining us on the squad."

I must have looked completely astonished, because he followed it up with a hefty slap on my back.

"Aren't you, Bro?"

I shrugged my stinging shoulder and said, "If you say so, Andy."

"I certainly do say so, Bro. The word's going in with the boss."

Then he clapped me on the knee with the palm of his hand.

"Tomorrow your super will be getting a call to push your transfer through."

"Jesus! That's fantastic. But what about that bloody exam, and the interview?"

"Come on, Rob," Andy said, irritably. "The word is going in. I'll push through a completed exam paper and fix up everything up with our DCI. With a bit of luck, next month you'll be on the team. Now get the fucking drinks in."

I sat there for a moment, speechless. I had been working hard for over a year for that exam, and now it had just been waved away.

"Hey guys, it's Rob's round. Isn't it, Bro?"

Andy handed me his empty glass.

"Yeah, sure. The next one's on me, guys."

Half a dozen empty glasses were simultaneously slammed on to the table in front of me. I hoped there would be a decent salary increase as a drug-squad DC. Otherwise, I couldn't afford the job. But just as I finished the thought, my brother leaned over and whispered in my ear, "Don't worry about the money, Bro. You're going to be making more loot than you've ever seen."

I had no idea what he was talking about – then. I must have had a really stupid look on my face. Andy just smiled and winked at me. And, as I sat there throwing down the beers and celebrating with Andy and his mates, I have to admit that I felt well avenged. But vengeance is at least an honest emotion.

These days, I don't get much that's honest.

# The Other Side

Jennifer watched the younger children playing in the sun. They screamed and laughed helplessly, running and falling, engines of perpetual motion. She watched the tub-like mothers who smoked and gossiped and watched their children grimly, martyrs to their blithe offspring.

She looked across between the tall, serried spearheads of the park fence and saw the men idling in loose knots on the pub corner. Her father stood with the group of men who were doing nothing. There was no work and nowhere to go, so they talked, and waved their arms around in the wind that blew up from the quelled docks.

They were all looking for jobs, but there were no jobs. Where were they, Jennifer wondered, where were the jobs? They were there once, but not one had been left behind. The men, like her father, had time to sell, but no-one wanted to buy it.

When she was a smaller girl, her mother had taken her to see her father at work, and she had realised that her father had a special kind of time to sell. Her father was a rescuer of things. He unlocked things, loosened them and set them free. The things he gave liberty to were all made of wood. Her father was a magician of wood, prying at its resinous captivity until it relinquished its treasures.

She remembered seeing her father hunched over, adroitly chiselling or assailing the wood with a volley of plane strokes. Her father could see inside the wood, he could see the things that she could not see, the things that lived there: the stools and tables and chairs. For a while, when she was very young, Jennifer thought that they paid her dad for his buckled back rather than his conspiratorial skills.

Now the men standing outside the pub were wasting their valuable time because the docks were closed. Jennifer didn't know why they had closed the docks, but her dad talked to her mother about 'the strike'. She thought that maybe 'the strike' had something to do with it. When she walked to the end of the street and gazed out at the dead concrete and silent wharves, she would look up at the quiet cranes that pointed skyward. Perhaps they were watching the sky for a crane Jesus, a transcendental Saviour of adamantine iron and case-hardened steel. Or perhaps the cranes

112

were now intent only on the sky's business instead of their own.

Jennifer noticed that the men had disappeared from outside the pub and the mothers were all drifting away, out of the park. It must be lunchtime, she thought, because that's what everyone did at lunchtime, they went home. Within minutes, nothing was moving in the dusty streets, except the dust. She climbed down from the friable back of the bench she had been sitting on and wandered towards the big iron gates.

Later, in the early evening, Jennifer would gather again with the girls in the park. They would sit on the swings, turning and twisting the chains that held the plastic seats and talk in low voices about boys and babies. Some of the girls' older sisters already had babies, though they hadn't had any weddings. But they didn't care. Nobody cared.

Some of the girls' sisters were prostitutes, or trying to be. Jennifer knew that prostitutes 'went' with men for money. But her friends' sisters weren't very good at it, apparently. They offered themselves to men for money, but the men didn't think they were worth it.

Jennifer listened to the other girls closely. They talked a lot about money, and about the things that money could buy. But to Jennifer money was just a word, because she'd never had any. At least, never more than the few

113

pennies her mother had let her keep for running up to the shops. But there was something Jennifer knew about money that the other girls did not: she knew that time was linked to money. She knew that time goes slow when you don't have any money. She knew that when there's no money around, time takes forever.

As the light faded and the girls chatted, Jennifer looked out across the dull waters of the docks, with their unobtrusive movements and their screaming birds that swooped and hovered. She wondered whether she'd ever get away from this place and these people. Would she ever leave the strained, rebuking streets of Splott? Would she ever get to the other place, the other side of the docks, where there was money, and time passed quickly and coolly?

She looked at the other girls in the gloaming light and knew that these people would try to hold her back, to keep her here amongst the sprawling, enforced indolence. Secretly, while sitting in the lengthening shadows with her friends, Jennifer would send her mind on a journey to the other side of the Bay – Goodbye! Farewell! God Bless!

"What do you think you'll do when you get there?" Jennifer's younger brother asked. She'd told him what she had been thinking about, about her thought adventures to the other side.

"I'll meet the nice people who live there. And eat the nice food they eat."

"Oh."

Her brother looked up at her with sad eyes, and meekly asked, "can I come with you?"

She put a reassuring arm around his shoulders.

"Course you can."

Jennifer understood quickly that it was a game that her brother couldn't play but she didn't have the heart to disappoint him. She knew that they had been excluded from something, that something was being withheld from them. Perhaps it was the salutary power of happiness that was being denied them, but she wasn't going to let that stop her.

Jennifer's teenage years were turbulent and tiring, but nothing much actually happened. She brought many misshapen feelings to bear on her family and home and the place where she lived. But she didn't surrender. She was still thinking, still doing, still trying. For a while, time stuttered and drawled for Jennifer, she didn't know what to make of time. She just worked on getting used to the idea, the idea of getting out.

Could she do it step by step, or would it be one big, chest-clutching leap, like jumping off a high-board at the swimming pool? Jennifer didn't really mind how it happened. She was

115

just waiting; and she knew that time was waiting too.

Meanwhile, her friends were beginning to people the world. But Jennifer wouldn't risk having a baby. Just the thought of the act made her wince with pain, and sadness. Only people who were in love should have babies.

One day, soon after the first appearance of her monthly bleed, her mother had tried to explain the rigours of conception to her. As she listened, Jennifer's mind leapt and thrashed, ignited in confusion and defiance. She wasn't going to let ANYONE do that to her. When her mother had finished her catalogue of regrettable arcanum, Jennifer bounded out of the house and ran down to the park. She sat on one of the hard benches for hours with her legs pulled up protectively against her chest.

Up until now, Jennifer had only ever thought about love as a game, or a trick. She thought that men weren't very good at love; she knew what love did to men. They thought that they could buy love with money, or with cars or with power. But Jennifer hoped that when she fell in love, money wouldn't matter, because when she had love she could swim out to where life is deep, and not be afraid.

Her evenings in the park were now spent leaning against a wall with the other girls. They puffed on cigarettes and sipped from bottles of cider. Boys would come and ask them if they wanted a kiss or a 'feel'. Jennifer shook her head every time, and they went away again. She discovered that she couldn't smoke, and she couldn't drink, unless she was drunk. And she knew for sure that she didn't want to be kissed or 'feeled'. When she went home, and was lying in her bed, she would say to herself:

"He's taking his time."

Sometimes she said it with tears in her eyes. She didn't try to staunch the tears herself. She wanted her prince to do it with a white handkerchief, the prince who was going to get her out.

"He'll come," she would say. And then blow her nose in her bed-sheet.


...So, what do we have here? A slice of Cardiff's regenerated dock-land. The straightened backs of stark and exemplary apartment buildings venture close to the water's edge. The tidal pools and barnacles have all disappeared, submerged beneath the steel-caged waters of a lagoon. The masculine browns of the mud-flats have been overwhelmed by the feminine-green displays of shyly rippling water.

A great eagerness is tearing at Jennifer. She has stayed up all the previous night thinking about the layout, thinking about what needs to be done, about the spiralling cost. The brochure has been unfolded and folded again and again. Now she is constantly smoothing down the rucks in her navy maternity frock and fussing

117

at the silk scarf she wears. It helps with her nerves. She is waiting, but she won't be waiting for much longer: the time has finally and joyously come.

Crossing to the window, Jennifer looks out over the Bay to where the old dock-lands once brooded. She can hardly see the network of terraced houses now. Beautiful new buildings array themselves between her and her old home across the water, buildings that glitter brilliantly in the sun, beckoning her to follow them into the audacious future.

She remembers how, when she was young, she wanted to see inside people's houses on this side of the Bay. How she wanted to shine a torch through their pretty windows and see how they lived their lives, to see their carpets and all the nice furniture that had been bought in a shop. She wanted to see them pick up books and read them, to smile at each other and talk without shouting or crying. She wanted to see them sleeping in the peaceful darkness, unregarding of the poverty that lurked across the deep scallop of water. But that was a long time ago, and time has moved on. Fortunately, time has taken Jennifer along with it.

The mobile phone in her handbag suddenly chimes into life.

"Hello."

A man's voice soundlessly crosses the airwaves, then bursts into sonorous vibrations in Jennifer's crouched ear. A question has been asked.

"Yes. I'm waiting for you at the apartment," she replies.

Again the man's voice vibrates in the tiny plastic cube.

"OK. See you soon."

And then, a reassuring:

"I love you too."

Turning back to the apartment, Jennifer absorbs the harmony of the living space, its clarity of design, its symmetry and rhythm. The right colours in the right places, the perfect proportions, the natural materials. And the light! The light is thick and eager, its photons bounding and twirling lasciviously, arcing through the air to fall as mute shadows on the polished-block floors. She feels that the entire apartment is expressive of her personality, her spontaneity and stylish discernment.

Jennifer rubs her eyes with her fists and then, bursting into a squeal of laughter opens them again. This is the pinnacle of her life. She feels whole at last. She is having the baby of the man she loves, and now he is on his way to look at their new apartment. The laughter has gone to her head; she speaks her name out loud.

"Jennifer…You did it. You did it!"

She closes her eyes again. She closes her eyes because she can feel it, the palpable present that hovers over her head. She can feel the present – feel it! Time can thrash and shout all it wants, but she is finally in the present. She begins to blink quickly with the heart-racing excitement of it all; she finally has it…finally has her LIFE! The feeling strikes her with its simplicity, its purity. She beams with the power of the present, and feels a little mad.

# Revenge

Shads' forehead was pressed up against the curved plastic; he was looking straight down the canted wing. He'd stopped listening to the odd banging and whining, the muted sounds of landing gear being prepared. He was almost home. Could he, by some miracle, get away with it?

At three thousand feet, the grim, overstuffed rain clouds looked as welcoming as his wife after he'd got home from a 3a.m. drinking session. Shads sat uncomfortably in the upright seat and looked out over the spread-eagled city. Cardiff was roughly a circle, he thought, its periphery Whitchurch, Grangetown, Ely, Llanrumney. The city was a circle stacked full of rectangles, arranged neatly into grids by a tidy god. Was it the same god that had allowed his baby son to die in the sickly tower of the Heath hospital? The same god that had allowed those murderous fucking medics to withdraw their life-giving treatment?

Shads no longer believed in any gods. After his son had died he'd turned his back on the cold Redeemer who had failed to answer his prayers. It was less a reaction to unanswered prayers, more a growing up: a realisation that god inflicted awful punishment on those who prayed too hard. Shads came to appreciate that everything was permitted by the catatonic Creator he'd gone begging to, as long as you didn't expect anything from Him. Good and evil were the same to Him, a truth of human – if not godly – nature.

So that stuff about god catching you when you fell – that meant nothing. When Shads realised this in its despondent entirety, he hit the stony ground of anti-theism: he'd become a strawberry-flavoured, chocolate-sauced, cherry-topped UN-FUCKING-BELIEVER. Since his baby died, Shads had lived in a dead and faithless world.

He remained with his forehead hard against the window, watching the city disappearing behind the tailplane of the aircraft. His stomach seemed to trickle from his belly to his legs as the plane dropped rapidly on its approach into Rhoose. He began to feel the discomfort of his distended bowel. The shift in his centre of gravity was moving the ten grams of crack cocaine that he'd wrapped in a condom and stuffed up his rectum. He began to sweat with the cramping pain, and the anxiety. He hoped,

122

with all his heart and his new CK underwear, that he could hold it in.

He wasn't smuggling the crack for his own use – are you kidding, are you fucking nuts? Don't you know how BAD that shit is? Don't you know how much that White Sunlight costs? Shads had tried a tiny piece of the junk in the Dam, just to make sure it was kosher, but six pints of lager and a couple of spliffs were his Saturday night bag. Fuck the coke. He wasn't even smuggling the stuff for profit, oh no. Shads was bringing an arse-full of crack-coke into the country for revenge. Elaborate, beautiful, gold-trimmed REVENGE.

When they landed, he would hang around the baggage hall until it got busy, then he'd saunter through customs with the irritable crowd. He was determined to get through, even if it meant hand-to-hand combat with the customs guys. It was vengeance that was driving him, blissful, sweet-as-honey and totally irrational. He squirmed painfully in his seat. It was beginning to feel like he had a bag-full of plumber's spanners shoved up his arse. His buttocks remained clamped rigidly to attention.

Thirty minutes later, enclosed in one of the airport toilet booths, Shads relaxed enough to feel the fullness of the ache in his large bowel. Five minutes after that, he had voided his precious motion and had washed the thatch of excrement from the smelly-precious package.

Every Monday morning, precisely at 10a.m., Shads would arrive at the University Hospital and make his way to Doctor MacDiarmid's office on the sixth floor. Every week the paediatrician's secretary would call security to have Shads removed. The good doctor had no intention of speaking to the dead child's father again, not if he could possibly avoid it. That wasn't part of the deal.

Dr Mac had done his best, as far as he was concerned. The baby had been three months prem. It wasn't his fault that the lungs hadn't fully developed. Difficult choices had to be made, resources had to be allocated. The baby was going to die anyway.

There was never any bother on those flagellating Monday mornings. Shads would just walk into the outer office where Dr Mac's secretary guarded the Senior Consultant's 'unavailable' presence. There he would politely ask the secretary if he could speak to Doctor Mac. She would then, equally politely, say: "I'm sorry, but Doctor MacDiarmid is not available this morning."

Then he would stand there, rigid and unmoving, until the poor woman would say wearily: "I'm afraid I'll have to ask you to leave." Shads would shake his head, almost imperceptibly, and the secretary would pick up the phone. Two minutes later Shads was being escorted from the building by two burly, blue-shirted, serge-trousered security guards. No, there was never any bother, even though Shads' brain hummed and vibrated on those excoriating occasions, even though his heart was torn and rent with lost fatherhood.

The rest of Shads' week was placid by comparison. The pain of Monday mornings telegraphed itself through his entire week, but by Saturday it had lost some of its razor-sharp definition. His Saturday night booze-up and the two joints he smoked were enough to decommission at least some of his anger, yanking him back from the murderous intent that constantly turned his stomach into purgatorial mush.

But on Mondays, the endless sequence of his self-immersion into the huge blender that tore at his grasp on reality and chopped his emotions into red cubes of psychosis, would have him raging again like a rogue elephant. He would take his revenge on the reluctant Doctor. Shads would ensure that the remote and elusive Senior Paediatrician would suffer some of the incurable, the corroding, the barbarising madness that was pulverising himself, his wife and his family.

On those nights he couldn't sleep; the nights he was overtaken with heart-rending rage, he would pad along the landing to the bedroom they had prepared for their son. His wife never made any attempt to stop him leaving their bed. The death of her baby had leached all the closeness she'd felt towards her husband, eroded and then retracted the affection they had shared. Shads thought perhaps it was the medication she was taking, the bottles neatly lined up, like a spice rack, in the bathroom.

While he shuffled to his son's bedroom, Shads would recall the moist orbs of his wife's eyes when she'd told him excitedly that she was pregnant. She was crying with happiness as she'd examined his face for a reaction. Now, her occasional, fleeting glance seemed to examine his face as though she was checking a tyre for its depth of tread. Six months ago, when Shads was a much younger man, his face had been handsome and engaging, but with bereavement came aching stress and affliction. The thwarted expectation of parent-hood slammed into him, bruising and distorting his face. These days, even the female eyes of the bloodless, smoke-wreathed hag behind the counter of his betting office gazed at him with more compassion, more morale-boosting synergy. He asked himself: what did his wife see through the out-of-focus cameras of her eyes – bitterness, rejection, her husband's face grotesquely twisted by a maddening hatred? Who could blame her if her look had become strange?

Even though they both wished for intimacy, too many other strong, intrusive emotions overtook them – the dark, tumultuous thrashings of the bereft. They'd given up hoping for bedtime cuddles and went to bed hoping only to dream of the little pink face that peered at them through the gloom.

Wasn't this whole business – the prioritizing, the husbanding of resources, the recalcitrant meting out of health-care – really about achieving government targets? Hadn't they used his baby son as a stepping stone to shining the shoes of some Whitehall mandarin? It didn't bear thinking about, but what else could he do? Think about the others who benefited from the space left by his six-week-old son? He wasn't that noble, that heroic, he didn't have it in him. He was full of something else though, something far less redeeming, less sublime: he was brim-full of something more immoral, spiteful, avenging.

Shads had his plan. He'd formulated his strategy weeks ago on a Monday morning as he was being customarily ejected from the hospital. He'd noticed that Dr Mac's secretary had followed them down to the reception area and then browsed the WRVS counter for a mid-morning snack. If that was her routine, it would give him the break he needed.

It would only take five minutes. The latch lock on the doctor's door would be no problem: his brief career as a jobbing burglar would help him spring it as easy as falling out of bed. He'd hide a bag of crack at the back of the doctor's

127

desk-drawer and drift out of the hospital like a chimera. Job done.

Dealing in crack-cocaine will get you a sentence that will halve your life-span: at least in the sunlit world. Using crack will get you nicked but probably cautioned, especially for a first time offence. But if you're a well respected Consultant Paediatrician, getting done for using Class A drugs will disintegrate your whole fucking career like you wouldn't believe.

You might have thought that Shads enjoyed planting the crack, but he didn't. In that office, he could feel the nearness of his Adversary, he could feel his numina, he blanched at the smell of the succubus. Shads felt the bile rising up into his mouth as he stashed the junk and fled from the room.

The FUN part came later, when he was ringing the hospital Chief Executive with a tip off – then the police, then the *Western Mail* and finally, for good measure, the reputation-drubbing *Sun*. Neat that.

As he stepped out of the phone booth, Shads' whimpering sorrow was shaping up nicely into a vigorous, feverish, day-and-night RETALIATION. Out in the early summer sun, he swung his arms nonchalantly as he joined the shirt-sleeved men and cotton-frocked women in their elaborate dance around the leafy square of the Hayes. He thought – and was vain enough to believe – that his plan would succeed, and that Dr MacDiarmid was about to have his imperturbable, unsuspecting head pulled through his arsehole.

The truth was that a drama was indeed about to take place in the sky-eclipsing tower of the University Hospital, but it wasn't the kind Shads had hoped for.

When Shads became aware that his plan had failed, nothing could diminish the despair, the resentment, the blind hatred he felt. He'd put his heart and soul into his reprisal plan – and it had COST him, big time. The malevolence he felt towards the doctor had now become cloven-hooved, Satanic.

The hospital administration hunkered down into self-preservation mode. They had instantly believed Dr MacDiarmid's protestations at being set up. There was even a prime suspect mentioned, of obvious predisposition. The police wanted to interview the assumed perpetrator. The press were informed, in an 'off the record' briefing, of the single-minded crank who had been stalking the doctor for months, harassing the impeccable, saintly, hardworking healer of children.

Shads remembered the last time he saw his baby son; wrapped up like a blind kitten in the ventilator. The poor mite looked as if he'd been sucked up by a see-through vacuum cleaner – all the pipes and hoses. He had felt like breaking into the plastic box and rescuing his baby, freeing him from the mayhem of the Special Care Baby Unit; he wanted to hug him, to take him home. That last time, Shads had hovered all night with his hand stroking the warm plexi-glass of the ventilator; the doctors had told him his son couldn't last for much longer: it was his lungs, they said; he was a fighter, but he couldn't possibly last much longer.

In the first moment of clarity he'd experienced since his baby died, Shads felt that nothing would ever diminish the pain he was going through. In that brief and terrible moment of self-awareness he watched his future tumble end over end, then burn up. The loss of his only child had scoured the life out of him. What could the rest of his life mean now? There would only be long years of tears and bitterness; long years to remind him of the son he had once so fleetingly loved.

As Shads pondered these shadowy thoughts, he heard a police siren racing through the cavernous streets and wondered if they were coming for him. He savoured his imminent arrest; he would enjoy the physical confrontation, the pounding of the truncheons, the punching and kicking. He would give the hireling fuckers a good run for their money.

To his surprise and disappointment, the cop-car swept past, on its inharmonious way to root out the misbehaving. As he trudged through the streets of the city's plexus, Shads looked up at the milky sky that hung over everything like a cataracted lens. He began to shake and tremble, then he let out an animal-like moan: long, loud, haunted. The painful sough from the bottom of his lungs brought him a desecrating revelation: Dr MacDiarmid, the pliant instrument of government, the plug-pulling, killer of babies, was about to rue the day he was born.

That night, lying in his dead son's room, Shads searched his mind for some repose. After a few hours of faltering sleep, he awoke, his feet cold, his joints aching as though they'd been hit with a crowbar, but the infernal smell of sulphur had left his nostrils. There, sodden with grief, he lay on the carpeted floor and wondered what his son's face would look like now; it had been more than three months and babies grow ridiculously fast. The boy had looked like his mother: black hair, dark eyes, upturned nose.

The agitation that drove him to rise from the floor was due only to his distended bladder. In the bathroom, while urinating into the bowl in a series of slow concentric circles, Shads imagined that he was pissing on the head of the man who had taken his son from him. Doctor Mac's mottled head appeared to Shads as a vulnerable egg, just waiting to be cracked. Squeezing off the flow, he stood, head bowed, until the nerve-chewing trembling began again. Drunk with anger, shit-faced with rage, Shads realised that his animosity towards the doctor was still poisoning him, draining him of his human spirit. But he didn't care.

"Why not?" he said silently, to himself. "Beating and torture would be too good for that baby-killing bastard."

Shads' thinking was becoming flamboyantly psychotic; he genuinely believed that Dr MacDiarmid was persecuting him. His arching mania searched for reasons why – why had Doctor Death murdered his son? The argument he alighted on was simple, but eye-bulgingly complex.

Shads' parents had been Jewish, though Shads himself never thought of himself as anything but Welsh; he'd never worn a yarmulke in his life. He wasn't a lapsed Jew, or a failed Jew; he saw himself as a Never-Was-Jew. But now, he seemed to absorb the full import of his Jewishness – the traditional persecution, the pogroms, the genocide.

What kind of name was MacDiarmid anyway? Dee-Arm-Ed. D-Ahmed. MacD'Ahmed. It sounded like an Arab name. A cold chill ran down Shads' spine. The persecuting doctor was standing in a long line of Mengeles, hunting down and murdering Jewish children. It was perfectly clear to Shads: Dr. MacD'Ahmed was an anti-Semitic doppelganger, and he would have to die.

"Ooooh," he moaned, "that'll do nicely." Shads was searching the internet. He had tapped the word PIPE BOMB into the search engine. It had thrown up eighteen sites. Now his middle finger hovered over the ENTER key. He hesitated for less than a second, then stabbed at the key like he was jabbing someone in the eye – BOOM! It was a goer. In some corner of his mind, Shads was longing to join his son.

As Dr MacDiarmid strolled across the hospital car park towards his new black Porsche, he smiled, appreciating the gleaming machine, it looked MEAN. But when Shads emerged from behind the bushes next to the car, he was looking a thousand times MEANER than the Nazi auto. He was wearing a back-to-front rucksack on his chest.

Shads pinned the astonished doctor against the side of the Porsche, his hand reaching for the length of nylon cord that dangled from his rucksack. He glared momentarily into the eyes of his terrified tormentor, then gave the cord a firm, strong tug. In a pico-second of roaring, flaming, hyper-expansion two lives were instantly and uselessly flushed down the toilet.

What was that? Shame? Yeah, you're right, of course it was a shame. But let me ask you something – and take a moment to answer – what would YOU do if the money-grubbing bastards pulled the plug on YOUR baby?

# Kevin's Youth

It was the Friday night drive home and the textures of the roadscape were fading into dusk as daylight succumbed to the unreality of yellow neon. A sudden downpour persuaded Kevin, the salesman (dental chairs), to interrupt the tyre-humming reverie of his long drive. He pulled off the road into the car-park of a Happy Eater restaurant. After switching off the engine and stretching his arms, he tugged at the rear-view mirror to check himself out. Loosening his tie then running his fingers through the gelled carapace of his too-long-for-the-times hair, he swanked at the approximate centre of the reflection.

"Nice to see you, kid. Looking goo-ood. Mid-life crisis my arse!" He was red-eyed from his drive and a long week working away from home but he still managed to crack what he called his 'film-star' smile. Though he bore the indelible marks of middle age – iron-grey flecks in the hair, the gloomy jowls – in his

135

mind still lurked that ludicrous furrow of postulating ego called 'his youth'.

In the restaurant's toilets, after a long and sonorous piss into the stainless steel urinal, he washed his hands and attempted to dry them in the intermittent gasps of fetid air that coughed bronchitically from a clapped-out drier on the wall. Leaving the toilets still waving his hands like a tic-tac man on a busy day at the races, he decided, as he usually had to in motorway-cafe toilets, to wipe his hands on his trousers.

In the days when Kevin was hitting his targets, when he was at the top of the dentist-chair sales tree, sticky hands would never have bothered him, he wouldn't have given those little frustrations the meagrest thought. Now, these lousy, messy, fucked-up, treacherous little affronts seemed to be consorting to turn his whole life into a lousy, messy, fucked-up, treacherous little TRAGEDY. Especially the treachery. Oh yeah – especially the treachery.

Last night, he'd humiliated himself at the Birmingham Posthouse, attempting to 'pull' the gnomic, fat-fingered, zealously perspiring barmaid. It wasn't that he actually fancied her – no fucking way, that shabby old bag, are you fucking nuts? – he was just trying to create his own entertainment, just trying to amuse himself after his meal and a bottle of over-priced plonk that courted being called a wine.

When he'd asked her if she fancied a drink back in his room, she'd unsmilingly told him to

"PISS OFF". He was conscious of her wide, white face and bulging, affront-sharpened eyes drilling into him for the rest of the night. He decided he was better off watching telly in his room. Walking down the endless carpet of the hotel corridors, he gave himself an internal memo – "Dear Kevin. Don't try fucking around with STRAY DOGS in future."

As he slid into a booth in the Happy Eater, he was thinking he'd be home in an hour, making strained, cheerless conversation with Claire and playing with the twins (it was Friday night, they'd still be up).

Kevin thought about the sexy Friday nights they'd enjoyed before the girls were born. He remembered how he'd sneak up behind his wife in the narrow kitchen and, cupping her breasts in his hands, nuzzle and kiss the nape of her neck until she moaned and went limp in his arms. Then, while still hooking the spikes of her nipples between forefingers and thumbs, he'd lower her to the cool tiles and bury his face in the tummock of soft brown curls that formed a perfect triangle between her legs, breathing in the heady, musky scent that stroked his senses like velvet fingers.

They'd be shedding bits of clothing in a yearning flurry of twisting, clasping arms and hungry misshapen mouths. His rapacious cock would be romping and bouncing about, looking for succour, until Claire homed its gouging head to the plump solace of her moistened labia. Then they'd make love greedily, the kitchen air adorned with the faintly sour smell of sex and spag bol.

When they'd finally broken free of the gravitational pull of their orgasms, they would roll helplessly away from each other, exhausted and starving for the half-cooked meal that sat furtively and voyeuristically on the stove.

If he tried to touch her tonight, he thought, she would probably shrivel at his touch. They were still sharing the same bed, but was it just a sleeping arrangement? Had his atonement helped to ease the fury of another betrayal, helped to douse the stacked and burning logs of treachery? Or was that strange withered scent that troubled him the funeral flames of his marriage? Tonight he would find out.

"Ready to order?" a silken voice was asking. Kevin primly folded his thoughts and looked up at the hovering waitress.

"Erm…tea, please. Er…and a tea-cake. Toasted."

"Honey or jam?"

The young waitress's hair was as black and shiny as a tuxedo's lapel, cut boyishly short, her hair throwing her waxy face into even greater contrast. She was dark-eyed and androgynously pretty. The slight turn-up in her nose made her look faunish, elfin. She cracked him a minimum-wage smile as she waited for an answer.

138

"Jam is fine." He treated her to an especially dazzling 'film star'. But she didn't seem to notice.

"Strawberry, blackcurrant or raspberry?"

"Mmmm…" He suddenly became conscious of an increased pressure in his loins, a slight fidgeting of the foreskin: the first little throb. By the time he'd said, "Strawberry, please" he was nurturing a full-blown hard-on through the worn cloth of his trouser pocket.

The waitress covered up the social manifesto of her smile and steamed away towards the serving counter. Kevin checked out the legs and rear end. She had a little girl's body, taut and fine-limbed like a Romanian gymnast. The skirt was nice and tight though it could be a bit shorter. Legs in and out at the right places. Her bum – no bigger than the average turnip – he felt he could have held it in the palm of one hand. Sequestered in the wistfulness of that dark, shiny skirt, the *gluteus maximus* of each cheek flexed and relaxed with syncopating genius as she walked. That bum had talent. That bum was going places. As she leaned across the counter, he pictured himself sneaking up behind her and…

He closed his eyes and thought hard; he was trying to draw her close to him using thought-transfer, ESP; he was trying to pull her using his mental fluids for sexual osmosis. Even in some dismal road-side cafe, he couldn't keep his sticky fingers out of the sweetness of the sugar-bowl.

The tea was cold and the tea-cake unappetising. Kevin looked again at his temptress. She was noisily chatting to the teenaged grill-chef.

Snotty little turd is probably BANGING her, he thought. Little bastard doesn't know what he's got. Two pokes and a bubble and it's all over for him. Her complete lack of interest in Kevin's winged thoughts mocked him. His erection had dissolved into a deep and turgid pool of scouring self-pity.

He felt like going over and giving the snooty little bitch a fucking good SHAGGING. Instead, he paid his bill and fussily tipped the faithless waitress. There were no more smiles. He could feel her adolescent indifference like background radiation. Over the last couple of days, vast acres of the lush rain-forest of his ego had been devastated, whole hillsides of his self-regard had been slashed and burned. He felt like getting drunk. No, that's not quite right, he felt like getting ABSOLUTELY-FUCKING -BABOON -ARSED - SHITFACED.

Relieved to be back in his car and on the move again, Kevin said out loud to no one in particular, "Think P-o-s-i-t-i-v-e!" His voice sounded authorial, knowing, like a voice-over on a 'How To' video: a 'How to be a

Materialistic, Miserable, Mendacious Bastard'
video. A 'How to Sit Around Jerking Yourself
and Everyone Else Off' video. He began to
swear every swear word he had ever known.
He began a stream of foul-mouthed profundity
that began with "Fucking Dogs…" and ended
with the self-immolating "…and fuck you too."
He felt better. But not much.

He was pulling off the M4 and on to the
A48(M) before he realised where he was. The
goading headlights of oncoming traffic had
failed to interrupt his stream of thoughts.
There'd be no smiles at home tonight either, no
spontaneous 'film stars' or homely pleasures.
Last weekend had been HORRENDOUS.
Claire had taken a phone call from one of the
female sales reps. Fiona had lobbed a grenade
into their Sunday lunch. In an ecstasy of tears,
she had told Claire about her six-month affair
with 'Kev'. She had then, nihilistically, gone
on to tell her how 'Kev' had just dumped her
for his new girl – that tarty bitch in accounts.

He swore that the humbling of last weekend
had taken fifteen years off his fucking life. But
he'd finally managed to calm everything down
before he left on Monday. They'd talked all
through the night, sipping countless cups of
guiltily-made tea that constantly got cold;
they'd TALKED THINGS THROUGH.

What was it she had asked him? Yes, that
was it, why did he get married in the first
place? Someone to look after him, he answered

himself now, on the long meandering journey through adulthood; his wife would be a younger expression of his mother's love and attention. Besides, his wife would forestall the pressing question of parricide.

He had married to get closer to his mother and avoid killing his father?

In an instant he thought of himself as a child, catching a ball thrown by his mum. His marriage was an answer to the archaic Oedipal dilemma central to a son's life. But these ideas were vague in Kevin's mind, they couldn't find clarity in his porn-served sensitivities.

" Fuck the Old Girl? Oh come on! Gimme a break…I'm no Mother Fucker."

Claire was OK, he thought. She understood. It was just sex – it didn't mean a thing. Nothing at all. He couldn't help it, could he? It wasn't his fault. His hormones did it. He couldn't control his hormones, could he? It was nothing to do with her and the kids, was it? It wasn't a threat to them.

Claire was as good-as-gold, sound as a pound, she understood. No problemo. He'd straightened things out; talked her round like a slick TV commercial. Then he'd sent himself an internal memo – "DON'T GET FUCKING CAUGHT AGAIN."

Kevin was an avid golfer and he thought all the important lessons of life were contained in the three rules for the perfect golf swing.

    1.  Keep your head down.

2. Follow through.
3. Cheat like fuck.

When he pulled into his drive, he noticed there were no lights on in the house, not even the kitchen light, with its gravitational gleam, its lighthouse solace – it was always left on if he was late home.

"Christ," he muttered, "it's not that bloody late!"

As he walked to the house it came to him. "Ah, I get it. They're in bed. It's the cold shoulder treatment."

He took out his key and let himself into the darkened house. He marched straight towards the lounge and the drinks cabinet, whispering to himself, "Fuck 'em. If that's the way they want to play it."

He slapped the light-switch with the palm of his hand and slung his bag on the sofa. He made it to the drinks cabinet and dropped its heavy door. As he reached for the malt, his hand stopped in mid-air. Propped against the curved side of the whisky bottle was a white envelope, a small pale rectangle that managed instantly to pare down all his emotions to one: COMPLETE FUCKING PANIC.

Kevin started to sweat. Then he began blinking rapidly, trying desperately to wish away the four by three cliché that was about to pour out his wife's teary frustration and distress.

143

He was afraid. He knew what was in the envelope and he felt sick, he knew what the goodbye note would say. He could feel the bitterness seeping through the thin paper of the envelope, its neatly folded contents a limpid discourse on his 'SWANNING AROUND'.

The note would be crammed with the ignoble details of his anarchic life, the embarrassing horrors of his lopsided marriage. He felt the house was suddenly scowling at him. It had become cold, very cold; there was no hint of warmth or energy, not even the faintest vibration of other people. They'd left him.

He didn't touch the envelope, he just lifted the whisky from out behind it and spun the top off in one vicious twist of his wrist. He lifted the bottle to his lips and took several deep, satisfying gulps before he came up for air.

Slumping down into an armchair, he lifted the telephone from the side-table and dumped it in his lap.

"Her mother's," he sneered. "Got to be."

He started practising the speech he'd been rehearsing all week, polishing his alibis, honing the Shibboleths of the deceitful. He was mentally threading and weaving his way like a slalom skier through all the accrued misdemeanours and tendentious lies. It'd be OK – he'd just have to slip up a gear from his usual shtick. He'd just have to do the biz, wouldn't he, he'd just have to haemorrhage some of his exuberant charm.

*Hey, Nix Problemo*. She'd come around. Didn't she always?

"Let it ring, Mum," Claire called towards her mother's bedroom. She was wise to all his moves, all his solipsistic attempts at excuses and manufactured poultices. "Take it off the hook."

She lay cosily between the freshly-bathed twins, snuffling the warmth of their soap-smelling bodies. She felt snug and reassured. She felt safe.

Her mother was padding down the stairs to unplug the still ringing phones in the kitchen and lounge. There would be no more phones ringing in her house for a while, not until her daughter regained some strength and balance.

Claire tried to think of a new life for her and the girls, a different kind of life to the one Kevin had constantly looted and ransacked.

She'd long ago given up expecting marriage to work, but despite the cynical despair, and ignoring the expended faith of her present union, she found herself wondering if she'd ever marry again. She fell asleep imagining what it would be like to be married to an ADULT.

Kevin hung up and morosely drained the last mouthful of Scotch from the bottle. The ever ready, "FUCK 'EM" leapt again across his wronged, whisky-moistened lips. He put down

145

the empty bottle and picked up the phone again, quickly punching out the familiar numbers of the local massage parlour. It was Friday night – Debbie would be working. It was still ringing.

"Must be busy tonight."

Debbie was his favourite. "Pussy like a pipe-vice." The phone continued to ring. "Come on. Drop that dick and pick up the fucking phone."

Still it burped and burped.

"She finally did it," he murmured. A female voice came on the line:

"Hello, French Massage, Tracy speaking."

"Hi, is Debbie on tonight?" Kevin was fumbling in his bag for his shaving kit. He needed to spruce up. That Debbie was no dog, she was a class act.

"She's not on? Bugger. Erm… So who's got the biggest tits…?"

# Run!

Keith Skaggs is a hair-triggered, mainline criminal. Hell, we have no need of euphemisms here – Skaggsy is one BAD MOTHER-FUCKER. He once frolicked like a rapacious hyena amid the arid urban badlands between the Taff and Culverhouse Cross. Now he festers in Cardiff Gaol gnawing away at the epidermal layers of a ten-year wound. Even so, he still has a relentless appetite for trouble: violence and madness remain his forte. He's the main reason I'm saying…

"Fuck this. I'm getting too OLD for it."

Skaggsy was scum. He knew he was scum too, because the Echo had told him he was scum; even though they didn't know he was the particular scum that had thieved the TV and video from the handicapped kids' day centre. So, Skaggsy knew he was scum – and he didn't give a toss.

As far as criminality was concerned, Skaggsy was very democratic (in a Stalinist kind of

147

way). He sublimely believed that everyone was created equal, including handicapped kids, so he thieved from everyone, equally.

He based this dazzling epistemological prank on the natural relationship between wolves and sheep. Of course, Skaggsy saw himself as the lupine half of the relationship: ravenous, cunning, a credit to his greedy role models.

Skaggsy saw thieving as his job, his means of earning a living, his rightful pursuit of a profit (he was a great believer in the capitalist ethics of avidity and profit). His pluralist attitude to crime meant that nothing was too big or too small. If there was a profit in it (and it was illegal) it was Skaggsy's business. Car-theft, selling drugs, handling stolen goods, burglary, Skaggsy had broken enough back-door glass to be a one man *Kristallnacht*.

The only sort of crimes Skaggsy avoided were violence and rape. Violence, for him, was a hobby, not business. And as far as sex went, Skaggsy was never without a Squeeze. The men of violence and the rich are never without a Squeeze.

Some of the ghouls and baggy-clad habitués of the Non-Pol club (Skaggsy's favoured watering hole) spoke in whispers about him being mental. They were right. Skaggsy was responsible for a lot of pain. It was appropriate then, that a nurse, someone responsible for easing pain, should have been his downfall.

Gen is short for Genevieve. Skaggsy and Gen met on a hot July night in the A&E department over at the Infirmary. Skaggsy wasn't there as a customer, oh no. He was holding a drip-mat to the guy's face that he'd had to headbutt as punishment for dissing him over the pool table. That meeting with the nurse was accidental and significant. Skaggsy didn't know it, but Gen was to be the chink in his criminal armour. She was his destiny, she was his…Tyburn Tree.

Gen wasn't his usual type. She wasn't like Steph, for instance. Steph, with her blank, lumpen expression and her talentless love-making: willing yes, but talentless. The nurse's smile was real, her smile wasn't the cozening mask he was used to. The first thing he ever said to her was, "What time do you get off then, Florence?"

They had a good run. A very good run. Some people thought that being with Gen was good for Skaggsy, calmed him down.

Skaggsy was always on the lookout for wrongdoing, everywhere. He saw wrongdoing in his sleep. He saw wrongdoing as his only opportunity for self-improvement. Even when he was relaxing, he would be masterminding some fashionably vicious mugging of a pensioner, or some drug-crazed burglary that ended in an innocent householder getting battered with a baseball-bat. But after six months of living with Gen, Skaggsy set out

149

each night on his habitual pillaging, feeling tireder, older, much thinner. He had a hunger for his nurse that went way beyond lust; his belly would gurgle at the thought of her.

His usual attitude towards women was quintessentially Taliban. But Gen was different. Skaggsy stopped seeing the others and re-furnished her flat for her. The genuine Chinese carpet that arrived in the middle of the night had to be cut in half to get it to fit. Unfortunately, their little piece of domesticity couldn't last forever. Destiny was waiting.

Skaggsy worshipped Gen, but he still looked. He had just left the flat to wander down for fags and his *Racing Times*. Mikki was still a schoolgirl… sometimes. She already had a grip on men. She was young, blonde, with tits that expanded by the hour. It took Skaggsy a pico-second to decide. It wasn't long before it went nuclear and Gen was the fallout.

"But she's only a kid," she screamed.

"At least she can get her fucking legs over my shoulders when we do it."

Then he walked out. Of her night, her dreams, and he took two halves of carpet.

The next morning, Gen had her strategy: she called a policeman.

DCI Hope couldn't believe his luck.

"You'll have to come up with more than that, love. We need names, addresses, dates."

"I can give you all of that and more, like it's from the horse's mouth. Just make sure he doesn't find out who told you."

Two days later Skaggsy's life was a bomb-site.

The trial was a paradigm of police mendacity. After the judge's summing up Skaggsy felt lucky they had abolished hanging. How DCI Hope scintillated, preened, posed beautifully for the cameras. Even though Skaggsy had committed only half of them, all those 'taken into considerations' beefed up the detection rate like you wouldn't believe.

He would wait more than anyone. Once a week, bent forwards at the window, he looked and waited. With baffled impatience he'd wait. Then she'd arrive.

"You're the only one, Gen, the only one who ever comes. You love me, don't you, Gen?"

"Yes, Skaggsy. I love you."

"Yeah. I know."

Gen had assumed that her cooperation with the cops was a one-off, but DCI Hope had other ideas. He would stop off at the flat on his way home to his wife, just to make sure Gen wasn't lonely, wasn't missing out on anything, so to speak. Hope thought it was a joke, at Skaggsy's expense. Gen wasn't exactly happy about this arrangement, but she knew that Hope could still be useful – as protection.

During one of Hope's visits, Gen was closing the curtains on the orange-hued street when she noticed a writhing burp of cigarette smoke stretching itself from the darkness of a shop doorway. She didn't see the girl's shivering hand rising to her vengeful, indiscreet lips.

"It…It was a fucking enigma. Couldn't work it out."

Skaggsy was talking to his cellmate, trying to draw lessons, but he still couldn't work out what had happened, he still couldn't work out what went wrong. Until Steph's visit.

That night, Skaggsy lay sleepless in his bunk, contorted by the truth. Unblinking, like a reptile, he stared at a future of gratifying violence, extreme violence: a psychopathic pornography of violence.

He wanted to hurt every part of her, he wanted to split every atom that had ever thrummed in a single molecule of her. When it arrived, his revenge would engulf Gen like a crimson avenger, like a silver-mercury flash, like a Bowie knife. Skaggsy knew there would be no eye-for-an-eye on this one, there would be no equivalence. His revenge would be promiscuous, prodigal in its cruelty. On this one, he was going all the way.

She had only taken a few steps into the Visitors' Hall and she knew. Gen knew that he knew. From thirty feet away she felt the brutality bursting from his etiolated prison face. His toxic stare was polluting every molecule of air that it passed through. The hate in his eyes rushed at her like the pyroplastic death cloud of an erupting volcano.

Skaggsy cleared the table and was half way to her before the screws brought him down. She only just made it from the room. His screams – "Piece of shit!" – formed a queue in her mind, replaying themselves over and over like a terrible jingle.

Gen cried all night. She'd never cried like that before: her tears astonished her. They began as heavy, confessional tears, but then moved quickly to tears of fear. Tears of fear are not like other tears. Tears of fear jump from the eyes in a series of exhausting explosions; only nihilistic weariness stops the flow.

When she ran from the flat to the taxi, she carried one suitcase. It was all she was taking. She was still wiping her face as the taxi pulled away and headed for the station.

'What was that, love?' asked the taxi driver.

"Nothing," replied Gen. "I didn't say anything." She hadn't realised she'd spoken out loud.

"Oh. I thought you said something like, 'He'll kill me'."

A minute or so passed. The driver looked in the rear-view and added uncertainly, "Must have imagined it, eh?"

But Gen knew he couldn't imagine it; nobody could ever imagine Skaggsy's vengefulness. All those things he wanted to do to her, not even an angry Old Testament God could imagine it.

DCI Hope was a shrewd bastard: all corruption and contingency. He understood human behaviour. Paradoxically, he had laughed when he'd heard the joke about Skaggsy chasing Gen from the Visitors' Hall. He'd said something like, "Do him good to let off a bit of steam." He should have known better.

The joke made it even more difficult for Hope to understand what happened two years later, when he got home and found his wife. She was lying on the kitchen floor in her birthday suit, babbling like a mad woman and swimming in her own blood. Skaggsy had taken it into his head, again, to let off a bit of steam.

The near-destruction of Hope's wife was the perfect crime – perfect in the sense that Skaggsy didn't mind getting caught. In fact he wanted it. He wanted his brutality to be famed, eponymous, iconic. Skaggsy was aiming to be the brightest star in the nutters' universe. He'd finally crossed the line: Skaggsy was mutating. He was becoming less than human, slipping away at thirty two feet per second per second from being what a human being is. In terms of

154

evolution, Skaggsy had regressed; he'd become a cross-current: a menacing, violent, knuckle-walker.

I looked up into the twin explosions of Skaggsy's eyes, those dangerous blue, uranium-depleted eyes. I thought he'd finished his story for the fifteenth bloody time, but he was going on at full throttle again.

One of the lags once suffered a careless loss of self-preservation, absent-mindedly telling Skaggsy to "Keep your 'air on." Thank Christ they've got those nets stretched across the landings. The old troglodyte suffered some bad internal injuries. (We've nicknamed the poor bugger 'Bunjee'.)

Even though I'm bigger than him, there's no way I'm telling Skaggsy to zip it. Even inside he's a tyrant, appointing himself as convenor of the 'business opportunities' department whilst simultaneously undertaking many lucrative outside consultancies. The bastard's building an empire in here.

"Fragility and fear. Fragility and fear, mate. It's what turns me fucking on."

His lips are as thin as a paper-cut, his face as colourless as my own. As all our faces. We're all the same colour in here – the colour of stupidity. I must admit I'd panicked when they put Skaggsy in with me. I knew the kind of shit-head he was. I've met plenty like Skaggsy inside: he's a classic.

I hope Gen is OK. I liked the sound of Gen. Apart from her mistake in going to the cops, she seems a nice girl. I'm glad she got away, she was lucky, very lucky. This bloody nutter is enough to scare anyone to death, and I've got to lie down beneath the menacing volcano every night and listen to his boiling rages.

But not for much longer, thank God. Thank God? ...Christ that's rich! God must have dreamt up bastards like Skaggsy just to make sure no-one gets any fucking PEACE around here. Anyway, I just hope that Gen is OK. A nurse, eh? Mmm...those tight uniforms. Now there's a nice thought to try and sleep on.

# Davey's Oak

Davey thought that city trees were a joke. He felt sorry for them, with their sparse moth-grey leaves feebly gripping the anorexic branches that forked the sky like pallid veins. Most of them were nothing more than broken poles, fearful of further notching and slashing from the kids on the estate.

He had once seen a fully-grown oak tree in a field. It was on the annual Non-Pol Club outing to Barry. About a mile outside the sea-side town, the magnificent tree was standing alone in a field like a newly invented creature. A few sheep lay on the grass around the beautiful tree's huge girth, enjoying the leafy shade beneath its intricate arms. The tree made a vivid impression on the seven-year-old city boy. After the beheaded saplings of the council estate, the oak looked so tall and strong he thought it would easily outlast the concrete and glass of the sombre tower blocks that formed the foreground of his daily life.

As the bus was grinding past that enchanted field, he longed to lie under the protecting wings of the great tree, and sniff the dizzying air that blew up from the beaches, stuffing his nose with its salty molecules from the nearby sea.

Set free with the other boys among the tummocks of sand, the blizzard of cricket balls and the home-made kites, Davey's memory clung to the oak tree like iron filings to a magnet. He would never forget it.

Five years had passed since Davey had been overwhelmed by the living beauty of the oak tree. He sat with his mother in their seventh floor flat, both of them wearing overcoats to keep warm. His mother economized by switching the heating on only after dark.

Lowering clouds smeared the windows with their dripping fingers, the wind moaned like noisy plumbing; it was the evening after a violent autumn storm. Davey sat playing with the hard kernel of an acorn he'd swapped for a swig of Cola in the school playground. When his friend had told him it would grow into an oak tree, Davey would have given him anything for it. He knew exactly where he was going to plant it. The next day he took it to the chosen spot, praying for miracles and for sleeping atoms to leap to their duty of growth and renewal.

The ground in front of Davey's block of flats held its secret for a year and a half. Then, one spring day, a snub-nose of green cleaved the brown earth like the long snout of a curious mole. When Davey saw it he froze. His prayers had been answered. His oak tree, a tiny green wand, was pointing at him with all the redemptive promise of Michelangelo's Sistine finger.

He nurtured and protected his tree over the years, through summer drought and freezing snows. He watched over it like a worried father as it grew stronger, ring by dendro ring.

Today, as he takes his son to school before going off on his rounds as an overworked social worker, Davey passes what is now called by everyone 'Davey's Tree'. A few weeks ago, two newly hatched blackbirds greeted him from its branches as they mustered for their hungry, open-mouthed day. Their stiletto beaks spread wide, throats yellow as moonlight, exploding into a raucous "Me first!" whenever the adult bird came near. The cheeping birds moved about the tree like feathered puffs of brown smoke, pleasantly interrupting the background hum of city traffic, and reminding Davey of what being human is: the part of being human that is drawn from the greenery of trees and the music of birdsong, the simple but precious human pleasure that comes from nature. In the city, looted of nature's essence, he didn't get enough of what being human is.

He gripped his son's hand tightly as they walked towards the communal 'green' at the centre of the estate. Strolling past the banks of overflowing wheelie-bins, the discarded bits of furniture and the littered shrubbery, he felt the leaden-weight of boarded-up windows, the freight of vandalised litter-bins set on fire, the bright yellow plastic hanging like evil-looking day-glo stalactites. Davey recognised the environment-shredding symptoms of a disgruntled and bored population, the detritus of an over-populated, congested melting-pot.

Last November fifth, Davey and his son stood on this green watching the bonfire and fireworks. That night, Davey had realised he was getting old. Those things the kids were letting off weren't fireworks, they were out-and-out BOMBS. Fireworks didn't 'go off' any more, they EXPLODED with a genuinely terrifying blast about a split-second after the blue-touchpaper was lit. Davey had never seen anything like it. He'd had a screaming headache all night afterwards.

Now as he approached the play-area, he nodded a sign of recognition to the faded old lady – if you can call sixty-ish old – who sat on the bench by the kiddies' swings. She wore a man's pork-pie hat with a feather in its side and she sipped from a can of Special Brew. Every day she came to feed a pack of stray dogs with tit-bits from her carrier bag. She did this saying over and over to the tail-swinging mongrels: "You're my lovely boys. They'll never find us here, my lovely boys." (Even though most of her dog-babies were bitches.)

She smiled at Davey, and reached into her pocket for a tissue to wipe her lager-beaded chin. He wondered what sort of narrative she carried in her head, what sort of strange story involved her hiding out with her 'Lovely boys'?

The estate was going to seed, the blocks of flats wore a tired, shabby look; like most of their residents they'd seen better days. People were walking around hugging themselves in parkas and fleeces, and appeared not to notice they were in the middle of a summer; even when it was warm, it was still a perpetual winter on the estate. A lot of things were perpetual on the estates: the demons of deprivation, the rot of exclusion, the violence and crime that swirled around the streets like running water.

Davey knew that the people were simply hugging themselves for comfort; hugging their addictions and delusions, their anxieties and hard-won lessons. Their lives were drenched in hardship like a great storm of poverty had just swept past.

Poverty had seemed to settle on them like an illness; it was intimate, a part of themselves. He resented the accident of being born into this bleak milieu. He felt himself too upbeat, too constructive, too hopeful, for the estates. He often said to himself, "I can do better than this." But deep in his heart he knew he belonged here, in the borderlands, in the great democracy of the unemployed, the unsatisfied and the unhinged.

As Davey passed by one of the ground-floor flats, he heard the brassy blast of a military march; he recognised it as the Dambusters' March coming from old Barney's open window. Suddenly Barney appeared at the window wearing a leather flying helmet and goggles, a silk scarf jauntily knotted at his throat. When he saw Davey and his son, Barney's arm shot out, thumb upwardly rigid.

"It's a bomber's moon, Davey," the old man called out. "We'll be flying tonight!" Barney had served as a Bevin Boy during the war; he'd spent five years underground, but always felt he should have been flying bombers. He'd bought the helmet and goggles in a pawn-shop.

Davey grinned at his son's wide-eyed astonishment, then called back, "Chocks away, Barney. Have a safe trip, mate."

The old man smiled, nodded, then disappeared back into the cockpit of his derring-do dreams.

Davey waved to the now empty window and walked on. All-giving smiles like Barney's were hard to come by. They were getting rarer; they were being scissored out of the cityscape, maybe to make room for the more fashionable grimace and sullen sneer of the upwardly mobile.

In the sixties, the new flats had come as a gift-wrapped blessing to the grateful residents who fled the nearby grid of crumbling Victorian terraces. The flats were small – two bedrooms, a kitchenette, a lounge that led on to a tiny balcony the size of a mouse mat. They were so small that a budgie's fart could be heard two doors away:

"You're not feeding that bloody bird wholemeal bread again are you?"

Now, forty years later, the residents had had a mood-change. They complained ferociously about living in the concrete shanty-town of the estate. The younger families had leaked away. Only puddles of twilight humanity lived here now, rooted in the estate's dog-shit-mulched soil: old age pensioners like petrified human remains, economic migrants, single-mothers. Social work and home helps were the thriving industries of the estate.

As he walked, he could feel that eyes were watching him from the towering blocks of flats, now shimmering like dirty, prefabricated waterfalls in the slanting sun. Those otherworldly eyes were going nowhere. All they could do was watch and wonder. Davey could see his audience perfectly, even though they were hidden. He could see them all too well.

He knew that many of the eyes watching him were weeping, though there would be no tears. There was no point in tears; tears were useless here. They didn't need his tears either, but Davey had wept many times for them. He loved these tricky people, with their flat-earths, their ambiguous reality and engendering smiles. His people, the flummoxed, the phobic, the fallible, who couldn't find a place for themselves in the competitive lattice of the Information Age.

Only those with money could afford information, only those with power could use it and, whatever the money-making game was, these out-of-focus people were never going to be players. They couldn't find a place among the striving and successful. The future was rolling away from them, so they became the apostate and everyone else was the enemy. Davey watched them scurrying from the newsagents, clutching their fags, their cider and their lottery dreams, hurrying to get home and shut the door on the functioning world like fearful agoraphobics. They saw the world through the ersatz glow of television 'reality'; going out into the real world gave them butterflies.

Sometimes Davey felt trapped like some endlessly repeating Lone Ranger, solving everyone's problems and dealing with all the variations of broken lives. Sometimes he felt he should be given time off for good behaviour.

But today the sun was shining and Davey was in a FUN mood. He tousled the wavy hair of his son as they walked. The boy tilted his head away at the sudden caress. To Davey's relief his son had inherited the dark eyes and good looks of his mother.

As they descended into the underpass, the smell of stale urine hammered at their noses. They walked, trying only to exhale, their oxygen-starved eyes begging for the light. Davey glowered at the broken bottles and crushed beer cans. He blanched at the cold, glinting needles that had recently passed a chemical heft through their sympathetic eye into the glad arms of heroin addicts. He hated what the drug dealers were doing to his people. He hated their BMWs and conspicuous wealth, their violence. To Davey, the underpass was what the end of the world would look like. His knotted brow advertised his rising anger. His fiery forehead glowed with indignation, with the rage and sadness at seeing that this pathetic worm-hole was for some people what being human had become.

Out in the sunshine again, the air poured into their lungs in a restorative stream. The world had not ended, and back beyond the slippery cave of the underpass, the oak tree was busily sucking up the city's pollution and easing sunlight into brush strokes of photosynthetic green, its shimmering leaves pleasing the eye like ten thousand miniature Picassos.

The tree will live on long after Davey, its great arms tilting in the wind like Davey's creaking ghost. And when, inevitably, at some future time, a greedy developer or rampaging road-widener rips the green lung from the rooted ground, the thoughtful of the city will howl with grief. Inside its growing trunk, the fragility of a living thing trembles, its deep and resinous heart forgiving all the things that we, ourselves, fail to forgive.

# Wales Forever?

Above the whitewashed houses of the town, the silken silence is shattered by the thudding blades of helicopter gun-ships. Their angry arms are tearing the thin air apart. The orange plumes of rockets are drawn down to the town at blinding speed. Everything is surrendered to the laughing flames, their vengefulness spread by a parching wind. The little hospital is destroyed, its rubble sprawled in the road like an accident victim.

The Kurdish people are on the move. Hand in hand they wind in a column through the hills, threading in a tired and broken helix through the gaunt valleys, the children feebly gripping, old men stumbling and falling, the women's faces notched with tears. Above them Saddam's hawks are wheeling, searching for their prey.

"I am happy," Omar said to Ilana. Her luminous face expanded into a grin. I am happy is all he can say for now and it is enough. They

167

have finally crossed the Channel. In the half-darkness he touches her hand. Her hair is tied with a red ribbon. On the morning they ran from the hospital, she adorned herself with a red ribbon, and freedom.

Through the creeping dimness, Ilana looks like a Giotto painting: angelic, not of humanity and its works. It would be easy to imagine her emerging from a four hundred-year-old sleep, the layers of time stripped from her face by a loving restorer's low light. She looks like an angel that has been lifted from the past.

They had never heard of Wales. Out of nowhere Wales arrived in their lives and they in it. They were surprised at the gentleness of the landscape; even the mountains appeared as plump and rounded as a child's fist. This Wales had a human landscape; there was tenderness in its plodding hills and wide valleys.

The country had an infinity of green, a multitude of shades that strived to say something intimate: something they were anxious to hear. The austere beauty of their homeland, airy and empty, would not deign to lend its lordly grandeur to human happiness. Their homeland, where they might never be again, stretched across their eyelids, sucking at them like a hungry whirlpool.

From the block of council flats, they could see hillsides behind the city. In the setting sun's purple glory, the hills seemed to smile like the faces of precious friends. As the shadows lengthened, they had a picture in their minds of the solemn hills of Kurdistan: strangely colourless grey and overexposed red, burnt by the sun as bright and sterile as a hospital. The sun of Kurdistan drills at one's skull, trepanning the bone with its crude, blast-furnace heat.

The council had put them on the top floor of the tower-block; it was like living on a hilltop. Perhaps they did it to make them feel at home. When she realised that there were no cellars in the blocks of flats, Ilana thought it was because no-one here needed to hide.

The view from their window was filled with the repeated clusters of pine trees, a green haze shimmering on the horizon, ridged with shadow like an Army-surplus jacket. The stillness in the flat was broken only by the homeless traffic down in the street, suddenly arriving and speeding away, seeking new dreams, perhaps looking for the peace that's too good to be true. The sound of heavy lorries rose to them like the thunder of a river, curving the air with an undulating rumble. The city air was filled with the traffic's buzzing, like the sound of distant helicopters, though no bombs fell from these innocent skies.

The postman passed by their door every day. They waited with a vague excitement, knowing there would never be any letters from Kurdistan.

Though the postman always smiled, their daily disappointment made them feel even more lonely, even more isolated. Ilana became obsessed with the arrival of the postman; she watched the clock and waited for him, with his heavy footfall and hopeful bag of other people's mail. The postman's name was Gwyn – he said it meant 'white'. When Gwyn stopped to chat, they would speak openly of many things, talking like free people talk.

Omar and Ilana bought a dictionary to help them with the language of Wales. Each day they would show a word to Gwyn the postman and he would tell them how to say it. The first words they learnt were *rhyddid, gweriniath* and *urddas*. Wonderful words, words that slid from the tongue like a sacred hymn; words that meant something here. When they spoke those words, Gwyn shook their hands and taught them the word *cyfaill*. Ilana could not pronounce any of the words. Her efforts made Omar laugh, and love, until he cried.

At night, on the grass behind the blocks of flats that squatted like concrete giants, the couple would sit and watch the stellar sky, looking for familiar points of light. But the darkness was always tinted by the splash of fizzing street lights. Starlight could not get in, turned back at Earth's giant borders.

Even so, Omar liked this place, this Wales. He liked living in his pseudo-hilltop home, as snug as a mother's lap, where the wind moaned like a sorrowful violin and the rain fell in a polite queue of tiny droplets. The rain here settled gently on his shoulders. Where he came from, the rain was a kind of sob, heavy tears slanting and scratching at the window's shield.

Cardiff's dull skies were sometimes weakened by a pampering sun, staring like a watery eye through the brightening clouds. In this country, the winter was a season that imagined itself as a wrinkle in a long summer. Even the weather's violence was softer here.

"What you need is lots of fresh air," Omar would say to his wife when she longed for the old home. "Exile is our destiny. But out in the countryside, we're refugees from pollution, so let's enjoy it!"

They would set off from Ely to take long walks in the fields north of the city. As they crossed the tightly embracing carriageways of the A48, Omar would recite the name of the place where they now lived: Ely. EE – LEE, Ee, lea. Ely. What did the word mean? What did the name imply? A hill? A hollow? A meaningless sound? In Kurdish, Omar thought, it would mean something complex and precise, like: every morning I need a cuddle. Or, I shall paint the front door then I shall vanquish my enemies. He did need a cuddle every morning,

171

Omar realised, as he laid a hand gently on his wife's shoulder.

"You were crying in your sleep again last night," he said.

"It's the nightmares," Ilana replied wearily. "I can't stop them."

Through the hills and fields and through the woods they would stroll, following the river valley to St. Fagans. In spring, they would wander across the drifts of blue-bells and past the yawning tulips, Ilana singing a Kurdish love song as she walked. It was always a sad song, in indignant exile like herself. Ilana's eyes would gleam, incapable of being dimmed, but her face was pale and sorrowing, like a drowning face.

One night, in bed, Ilana asked Omar if they would stay in Wales forever.

...FOREVER!

A concept that was too huge and raw to swallow clenched at the back of Omar's throat.

"I would like to go home too," he finally answered, turning his face to hers.

Her tears crashed like a wave that had finally broken, flowed from holes that couldn't be plugged. They became Omar's tears. Face to face they shared their salty ache, enduring together. The forsaken corpse of their homeland lay between them, slaughtered by an insane gangster.

Omar watched his wife until her tears stopped and her breathing slowed, until she was asleep. Then he rose and moved to the window. The surrounding blocks of flats rose into the moonlight like white, slab-sided stalagmites. Even though he'd never seen an iceberg, he imagined the pale monoliths as icebergs floating in a smoky sea. The streetlights were trying to overcome the yellow moon-glow with their scorching orange. He was already tired of the neon novelty, of the immensity of garish photons chasing the darkness through the streets and melting it into eerie shadows.

An ache filled the back of his throat, his chest felt hollow and haunted with voices from the past. It wasn't weariness that drove him back to bed; his embittered thoughts reeled around his brain at the speed of light, making him dizzy.

He wanted to hold Ilana close, he wanted to cling to her to stop himself falling down some precipitous slope. Her exhausted, gratefully horizontal body now slept with child-like intensity, rocked to sleep by her terrible sobs.

Omar hoped that his wife would sleep soundly through the night. Lately, Ilana had begun whimpering and grinding her teeth in her sleep. Then she would wake, thrashing and moaning from a terrifying dream. Whatever psychological problems were hunting her down, he would subsume her anguish with all the love he could conceive; his love would be like a chair following close behind her, keeping her from falling.

He breathed in her warm scent, sensual and comforting like the smell of vanilla. In the street a heavy lorry groaned its way up the hill as he searched his mind for sleep. He wondered if FOREVER had begun.

The next morning, Omar found that someone had sprayed graffiti along the crumbling wall of their block of flats. In large red letters it said...

CROESO – OUR COUNTRY ENFOLDS
YOU IN ITS ARMS.

Omar was astonished. Gwyn had only recently told him, in one of their discussions, that nothing turns a man into a Nazi quicker than an immigrant getting ahead of him on the council housing list.

He leaned his cheek against the wall and cried. At last. At last he felt safe. Perhaps, he thought, among the world of nations a country should be known by its graffiti.

In Kurdistan, Omar and Ilana had been the doctor and nurse of the town's little hospital. They discovered, happily, that their medical skills were badly needed in their new country. Omar is now retraining to practise paediatric medicine and Ilana nurses at the University Hospital. She now cares for the sick people of

Cardiff like the city once cared for them. They see it as a circle of giving and receiving, like all of life.

From the time that the tough men of the Legions arrived from Italy, Cardiff has been a place that has always said: "Welcome stranger, you bring us new ideas. Come on in!"

# Blind Date

You know the deal: divorced, on my own, financially vivisected; living in a body-bag of a flat above a takeaway. The smell and the noise! It's like living in my underpants. That divorce really did a whammy on me. I'm not kidding. But it's no use weeping just because you've been dumped on, right?

She made the smart move, my ex; she did the right thing – defected. I don't blame her, she was just looking out for herself, just taking care of business. The other guy had a full-time job for Chrissakes, a superannuated nine-to-fiver. I just wish things could have been different. I'm missing her like hell. I miss her voice, her company, her omniscience; I miss the sex and a clean coffee mug.

When she told me she was leaving me for another guy, regrettably I said:

"Go ahead, it's a free country. Do what you want."

When what I really meant was – 'Please don't do this. Please don't go.'

She obviously wasn't listening; she wasn't reading the sub-text. I can't believe a smart girl like her couldn't read between the lines. You know I never really understood how we two got together. We were as different as the two poles on a magnet. She was intelligent, mature, sane, I wasn't.

They're great fun, those Lonely Hearts: the purple, the wounded hearts. Everybody reads them. Everybody loves the insanity of people trying to make themselves sound attractive. Nearly everyone living on their own tries their hand at them, sometime or other. I often thought about how my own ad should read – fortyish, balding, mad, slashed to the core by life. Hobbies: booze, smoking dope, masturbation.

What do you think? Think I'd get a date? Why not? There are hundreds of guys like me out there, thousands of guys. Without guys like me there'd be no lonely hearts. Of course, I always check out the women's column as soon as I pick up the paper. OK, I admit, I'm desperate for some company.

I've been pretty hopeless lately. I've stayed drunk for six months. You'll be happy to know that I'm an excellent drunk; I really do excel at it. Getting boozed up is my main hobby, my chief racket right now. But at least I'm cutting back on the ganja smoking. I've been getting too many chest infections. It's got so bad, that every time I pull a mouth-full of smoke the *No Smoking* sign goes on in my lungs and I have to cough it back out.

My lungs know how to handle themselves; they keep those tubes spick and span. But two doors down from my lungs, on the next landing, there's a riot going on in my liver. They're burning and looting down there. Then there's my kidneys. Oh boy, my kidneys are really feeling their age. Right now, my kidneys are Palaeolithic.

Yeah, I know, I know, I need help. I know what I've got to do. I've got to get into another relationship; I need a real live woman to squeeze instead of a bottle. I know I need help. But I don't suppose I've got much of a chance with women, looking and feeling like I do.

What is it with women and the booze thing anyway; why do they have such a downer on us drunks? Why have they got to feel so incredulously wounded about a guy getting shit-faced for most of his time? Just because we have to crash out on someone's floor occasionally, is that a crime? What is it about a guy getting ratted or giving himself a hand-job that gets women so pissed off? Why are they so bloody unreasonable?

...I still can't believe she's gone; I've been spectacularly depressed since she left.

Now I think my knees have a disease. This degeneration is something new; this enemy-within just sneaked up on me. Pain is trying out new tunes on me; wandering up and down the xylophone of my spine with its petulant hammers. Here's a malicious little number – I only have to try and get up from a chair and my knees crack like glass; they make a sound like beer bottles shattering. My head and my knees hurt all the time. Christ, I'm getting old.

Vicky sounded great.

'...*attractive blonde'*, then I read, '... *wishes to meet artistically inclined...'*

Oh Jesus. Vicky, give us a break, pleeease. They're all bloody whackos. Forget artistic, randy old Picasso is dead and Damien Hirst would have your cat sawn in half and swimming around in formaldehyde before you could say 'here pussy-pussy'. Artistically inclined... my arse. Forget it.

I can't believe I'm doing this. You know, none of this would have happened a year ago. But I'm forty now, that's probably why I'm doing it. The world and me are getting older; the world and me are headed for the old folks' home. I wonder if the world is getting lonelier. I mean, with everything flying apart in an inflating universe, things are going to get a bit isolated around here. Pretty soon the world won't be seeing much of anything, just a big black empty socket, a lonely scalloped sky. The world and me – my pal the world and me – are getting older, lonelier, sicker. And looking at these lonely-heart ads, it seems that everyone else is trying to get in on the act.

So now I'm standing outside the Queens; freshly showered, clean-jeaned and best-jacketed. I'm waiting. My face is getting slapped by the unimpressed city rain. I'm watching the crowds pass. Have you noticed that there is no finesse in the city at night, no manners, no give-and-take? The city at night turns selfish: it's all take.

Tell me something: why is it the young are always on the button where fashion is concerned? How come the young always understand fashion? I tune in to the whimpering of my white socks – they know they are way off the beam. They seem to sway around as they cling to my feet. They seem to be ducking, trying to hide. Truth is that I was never a contender in the fashion stakes. Fashion always seemed to be sniggering at me behind its hand.

Some of these pranksters that pass by are wearing footwear that cost four or five times what I got for the best poem I ever wrote. That's three months of beating my brains out for half a sole on a sports trainer. Not even a whole bloody shoe, for Chrissakes!

That sounds fair enough, doesn't it? That's putting art where it belongs: under the heel of some yob. That just about sums it up, doesn't it? That means there is absolutely no irony when some pin-brained politician talks about 'yob culture'. It means there is absolutely no contradiction at all. Try mentioning culture to a politician without the 'yob' epithet and, unlike the old Reichsmarschall, they no longer reach for their revolvers – these culture-sucking bastards are picking up twelve-bore shotguns.

The city's demographics are re-shuffled at night. The street population is sieved and filtered until only the young remain; a laughing, violent sediment. The crowds come in from the estates, from the Indian Territories, in convoys of whacked-out GTi's and RX's with jumbo-spoilers and ear-drum blistering stereos that make your lungs reverberate as they cruise past.

You can see them in gangs, prancing and flailing through the night-time streets: groups of go-go-girls and go-ded boys. The haunchy, chip-shop-fed girls with glittered faces glowing like electric rashes, showing huge acreages of flesh that speak of sexual praxis and teen-coital know-how.

The boys, secure and muscular in their youth, bristle and burp, watching the women and slyly checking themselves out in every shop window. Checking that every tattooed skull and bleeding dagger is exposed and athletic. These 'boys' have a talent for giving grief, a facility for the joyous application of violence: for fucking people over.

I am getting old and sick: I'm as neurotic as a poodle. There's too much happening on the city streets at night; too much damage and pain, too many incidents. The night-time streets scare the hell out of me. Yep – these lads flying the black flag; these shave-headed, kebab-hefting, bottle-sucking pogo-ists scare the shit out of me. Each one with his retained probation officer and duty solicitor; each one on first name terms with his personal excuser and pleader. These kids make me feel like an antique – something small and fragile – like something made in Meissen. No wonder they're all narced-out on something; they're probably scared shitless of each other. I was never any good in a rumble and now I'm too old to make a run for it.

Why the hell did she want to meet here, in the city centre – in the War Zone? And in the cauldron of the Queens! Yeah – that's right. I'm waiting for Vicky. Well? …I'm artistic. I'm a bloody poet, for Chrissake.

She could have picked somewhere better than the Queens though, the place is a zoo; full of pterodactyls and hellhounds. She's late. Good. I can bugger off home. I'm going…now…Jesus, is this her? Wow – what a smile! I'm staying.

Hell, this is good news. This is good news. She's gorgeous; she's a genuine page three pin-up, a jaw-dropping Kylie-fucking-Minogue.

She's walking towards me holding out her hand.

"Dennis?" she says. I slip her my trembling, pulse-quickened grip.

"No shit – that's my name too." Five minutes later, and she's still struggling to free her herself from my unbelievingly grateful, desperately pleading hand-clasp.

The polished brass and teak of the Queens is the sort of place where the money-men, the execs, the brief-case brigade, love to 'do lunch'. But at night, the clubbing clientele takes over, dealing and trafficking in chemicals and poisons to the sniffers and poppers, the shooters and droppers.

Down at the churchyard, where the winos hob-nob in their grotto, it's like a detox clinic compared to all the shit that goes down in the pubs and clubs. Down at the churchyard, those guys are highbrow sherry sippers. To be honest, the churchyard is where people like me belong. I feel at home with the alcos and the Dostoyevskian citizenry – the "rag and bone men" in their "dirty and stinking courtyards". The morbific murderer Raskolnikov discovered that cities have a penchant for blood and human carrion. He understood that poverty and city gloom is enough to make anyone want to whack some poor granny.

In the Queens, high-energy karaoke pummels and warps the smoky fug into a crumpled coma. Clutches of 'hens' swear loudly and burn the scorched air with the latest molten rock-tune, scandalising a microphone that gets passed from hand to sweaty hand; squeezing and torturing it like some recalcitrant dick.

So, shit happens – to me. And usually, I can't even prepare myself. The awful thing is, it just happens. When I came to, I mean when I regained consciousness, I was lying on a trolley in a brightly lit corridor with a young nurse hanging over me and asking if I could feel any pain. Oh Christ could I feel pain. I was all pain. As far as feeling pain was concerned, I was upwardly mobile. What happened to me? Well, I'm not at all clear about it, but I'll tell you later what the police told me happened.

Here it comes – here's the joke: fortyish bloke goes on blind date and meets a gorgeous, blonde, pert-breasted young woman in her mid-twenties. Good joke, huh? Well, it's true. It happened. Like I said – shit happens, to me. Oh yeah, I mean shit happens alright.

Vicky was film-star – authentic centre-fold. As we sat down with our drinks, I began to take her in, began to sweat pheromones and get as rigid as a didgereedoo. I felt the rush of blood from my brain to my groin; I thought I might pass out.

This girl was permanent hard-on, a walking talking sex-fest. She was wearing a palm-chafing black number that was as tight as a violin string. Her make-up was light and happy, not like that heavy misery kind you see on the make-up counter girls: the three hour renovating plaster job that you could play drumsticks on. She was heart-breakingly pretty, body-perfect and friendly. In my experience, you can tell all you need to know about a woman in the first thirty seconds.

Now I'm just an average bloke. I carry a bit of puppy-fat, I'm losing my hair and my face looks like a cracked walnut until you've had a few large ones. So I couldn't understand why this bombshell was smiling constantly and writhing against me like a porno-star on Viagra.

Hey – I'm not that lucky. And then it hit me. No, I mean it. The heavy glass ashtray off the bar hit me on the back of the head. So I took an unscheduled trip to la-la-land. You know where I woke up? Yeah – on a pain-shimmering trolley.

Ok, so this what they told me, this is what the cops said. Vicky had split with her boy friend, some kind of Cro-Magnon throwback that had knocked her around once too often. Anyway, for some mysterious reason she missed him and wanted to get him back. And here's the big idea, here's the Lady Macbeth: she thought she'd make him jealous so that he'd be the one to ask her back. He'd seen her canoodling up to me and decided to practice his frisby throwing

186

technique with that bloody ashtray at the back of my head.

I went out like a light. Someone had heard him shout, "Hey Grandad, that's my girl." After the ash tray struck its target, he strolled over and played footy with me until the cops arrived and called half-time. When they searched him they found a few tabs – his head was somewhere up in the troposphere.

You know what's really funny, you know what's so fucking hilarious about all this? That blind date almost blinded me. I lost my vision for two days; it just all blurred out. They thought my retinas might have detached themselves from something; it sounded like the paint job on the inside of my eyes was flaking off. For two days it felt like I was on drugs myself.

Here's a snaggy headline – *Ashtray Eliminates the Need to Take Drugs!* But thank Christ my sight came back. I wish they could do something about these bloody knees though; these Trojan Horse knees are not taking me seriously at all.

I don't know what to do about this lonely-heart thing. It's a problem. Here's what I've said in this ad I'm writing. I sound mildly attractive on paper.

…'thirty-something guy, likes kids & animals, handsome, artistically inclined, brill in the sack, would like to meet someone to sit on his face…'

Oh come on, I'm just being a precocious forty-year old here: I'm writing a cheque that will never be cashed – no one's going to reply. And I don't blame them. Would you go on a blind date with someone who placed an ad like that? You would…Jesus!

These things are not ads – they're not really advertisements. What are we advertising – loneliness, desperation? What are they really? These things are more like homages to our powers of expectancy, a triumph over the inevitability of repeating and bitter experience.

These things are like love letters to ourselves. We're declaring our worth, our belief that we are worth something, worthy of someone. We declare that we have things to give, things of value. But it's best not to think about what you're doing when you place one of these supplications. It feels like you've crossed a threshold, it feels like opening a door and letting some terrible longing in. It's like waking up at 4a.m. in an empty house, on an empty street, in an empty city – it's best not to think about it.

Anyway, what do you reckon…think I'd get a date? Well, I got lucky the last time, didn't I? That Vicky I mean…you don't agree? I don't either. Like I said, though, I'm desperate for a bit of company. A winner like you wouldn't know, but people like me are always a little

188

desperate for something. It's OK, don't worry about us; we're used to life giving us the V-sign. But we're fighting back. We're even taking out ads to show the world that we're fighting back. Check it out. Check it out.

# More Titles
# From Accent Press Ltd

**The Last Cut**                 F.M. Kay
ISBN 0954867378                  £6.99
A powerful and provocative collection of erotic poetry. Her
poetry pares emotions to the bone, exposing the pain and
exhilaration of an overwhelming affair.

**Remembering Judith**           Ruth Joseph
ISBN 1905170017                  £7.99
Written in memoir form, Ruth details the story of her mother
Judith's escape from Nazi Germany in 1939. The trauma caused
Judith to develop anorexia. Ruth's childhood is consumed by her
struggles to nurse her mother and cope with an abusive father,
within the rigid constraints of 1950s Britain. (Available Sept 05)

**The Boy I Love**               Marion Husband
ISBN 1905170009                  £6.99
A stunning, compelling debut novel set in the aftermath of WWI.
It explores the complexities of war hero Paul's homecoming.
Paul's choices have repercussions on several lives as he spins a
tangled web of love and betrayal. (Available July 05)

**An Eye of Death**              George Rees
ISBN 0954709276                  £7.99
This rip-roaring novel illuminates life in Tudor London at the
time of Shakespeare, Marlowe and Sir Walter Raleigh. Fast-
paced action, murder, intrigue, lust and treachery – breathtaking!

# Titles Available By Post

To order titles from Accent Press Ltd by post, simply complete this form and return to the address below, enclosing a cheque or postal order for the full amount plus £1 p&p per book.

| | TITLE | AUTHOR | PRICE |
|---|---|---|---|
| ☐ | Sexy Shorts for Christmas | Various | £6.99 |
| ☐ | Sexy Shorts for Lovers | Various | £6.99 |
| ☐ | Sexy Shorts for Summer | Various | £6.99 |
| ☐ | Scary Shorts for Halloween | Various | £6.99 |
| ☐ | Why Do You Overeat? | Zoë Harcombe | £9.99 |
| ☐ | How to Draw Cartoons | Brian Platt | £7.99 |
| ☐ | Notso Fatso | Walter Whichelow | £6.99 |
| ☐ | Triplet Tales | Hazel Cushion | £5.99 |
| ☐ | The Last Cut | F.M. Kay | £6.99 |
| ☐ | An Eye of Death | George Rees | £7.99 |

All prices correct at time of going to press. However the publisher reserves the right to change prices without prior notice.

PO Box 50, Pembroke Dock, Pembrokeshire, UK. SA72 6WY
Email: info@accentpress.co.uk     Tel: + 44 (0)1646 691389

Cheques made payable to Accent Press Ltd. Do not send cash. Credit/ debit cards are not accepted.

NAME _____

ADDRESS _____

POSTCODE _____